DOVER · THRIFT · EDITIONS

Humorous Stories and Sketches

MARK TWAIN

DOVER PUBLICATIONS, INC.
Mineola, New York

DOVER THRIFT EDITIONS

GENERAL EDITOR: STANLEY APPELBAUM
EDITOR OF THIS VOLUME: PHILIP SMITH

Bibliographical Note

This Dover edition, first published in 1996, is a new collection of stories, reprinted, unabridged, as they originally appeared in the following books and periodicals: "The Notorious Jumping Frog of Calaveras County," *Mark Twain's Sketches, New and Old* (The American Publishing Company, Hartford, 1875; the earliest version of this story was first published as "Jim Smiley and His Jumping Frog" in the New York *Saturday Press*, November 18, 1865); "Journalism in Tennessee," the Buffalo *Express*, September 4, 1869; "About Barbers," *Galaxy*, August 1871; "A Literary Nightmare," *Atlantic Monthly*, February 1876; "The Stolen White Elephant," *The Stolen White Elephant Etc.* (James R. Osgood and Company, Boston, 1882); "The Private History of a Campaign that Failed," *Century Magazine*, December 1885; "Fenimore Cooper's Literary Offences," *North American Review*, July 1895; "How to Tell a Story," *Youth's Companion*, October 3, 1895. A new introductory Note has been specially prepared for this edition.

Library of Congress Cataloging-in-Publication Data

Twain, Mark, 1835–1910.
 Humorous stories and sketches / Mark Twain : [edited by Philip Smith].
  p. cm. — (Dover thrift editions)
 Contents: The notorious jumping frog of Calaveras County — Journalism in Tennessee — About barbers — A literary nightmare — The stolen white elephant — A private history of the campaign that failed — Fenimore Cooper's literary offences — How to tell a story.
 ISBN 0-486-29279-7 (pbk.)
 I. Smith, Philip, 1967– . II. Title. III. Series.
PS1302.S54 1996
813'.4 — dc20
                   96-19752
                   CIP

Manufactured in the United States of America
Dover Publications, Inc., 31 East 2nd Street, Mineola, N.Y. 11501

Note

The outstanding humorist of the United States, Mark Twain (Samuel Langhorne Clemens, 1835–1910) attained tremendous popularity as a writer and speaker, beginning with the publication of the first version of his "The Notorious Jumping Frog of Calaveras County" in a New York newspaper in 1865. Twain's prolific output included novels, travel writings, stories and sketches. In all of these forms he excelled, infusing his narratives with a distinctive comic personality. This volume contains a selection of Twain's most noteworthy short humorous works, and illustrates the range of his writings.

Contents

(Dates are those of first publications.)

The Notorious Jumping Frog
of Calaveras County

IN COMPLIANCE WITH the request of a friend of mine, who wrote me
from the East, I called on good-natured, garrulous old Simon Wheeler,
and inquired after my friend's friend, Leonidas W. Smiley, as requested
to do, and I hereunto append the result. I have a lurking suspicion that
Leonidas W. Smiley is a myth; that my friend never knew such a personage; and that he only conjectured that if I asked old Wheeler about
him, it would remind him of his infamous *Jim* Smiley, and he would go
to work and bore me to death with some exasperating reminiscence of
him as long and as tedious as it should be useless to me. If that was the
design, it succeeded.

I found Simon Wheeler dozing comfortably by the bar-room stove
of the dilapidated tavern in the decayed mining camp of Angel's, and
I noticed that he was fat and bald-headed, and had an expression of
winning gentleness and simplicity upon his tranquil countenance. He
roused up, and gave me good day. I told him that a friend of mine had
commissioned me to make some inquiries about a cherished companion
of his boyhood named *Leonidas* W. Smiley—*Rev. Leonidas* W. Smiley,
a young minister of the Gospel, who he had heard was at one time a
resident of Angel's Camp. I added that if Mr. Wheeler could tell me
anything about this Rev. Leonidas W. Smiley, I would feel under many
obligations to him.

Simon Wheeler backed me into a corner and blockaded me there
with his chair, and then sat down and reeled off the monotonous narrative which follows this paragraph. He never smiled, he never frowned,

1

he never changed his voice from the gentle-flowing key to which he tuned his initial sentence, he never betrayed the slightest suspicion of enthusiasm; but all through the interminable narrative there ran a vein of impressive earnestness and sincerity, which showed me plainly that, so far from his imagining that there was anything ridiculous or funny about his story, he regarded it as a really important matter, and admired its two heroes as men of transcendent genius in *finesse*. I let him go on in his own way, and never interrupted him once.

"Rev. Leonidas W. H'm, Reverend Le—well, there was a feller here once by the name of *Jim* Smiley, in the winter of '49—or maybe it was the spring of '50—I don't recollect exactly, somehow, though what makes me think it was one or the other is because I remember the big flume warn't finished when he first come to the camp; but anyway, he was the curiousest man about always betting on anything that turned up you ever see, if he could get anybody to bet on the other side; and if he couldn't he'd change sides. Any way that suited the other man would suit *him*—any way just so's he got a bet, *he* was satisfied. But still he was lucky, uncommon lucky; he most always come out winner. He was always ready and laying for a chance; there couldn't be no solit'ry thing mentioned but that feller'd offer to bet on it, and take ary side you please, as I was just telling you. If there was a horse-race, you'd find him flush or you'd find him busted at the end of it; if there was a dog-fight, he'd bet on it; if there was a cat-fight, he'd bet on it; if there was a chicken-fight, he'd bet on it; why, if there was two birds setting on a fence, he would bet you which one would fly first; or if there was a camp-meeting, he would be there reg'lar to bet on Parson Walker, which he judged to be the best exhorter about here, and so he was too, and a good man. If he even see a straddle-bug start to go anywheres, he would bet you how long it would take him to get to—to wherever he was going to, and if you took him up, he would foller that straddle-bug to Mexico but what he would find out where he was bound for and how long he was on the road. Lots of the boys here has seen that Smiley, and can tell you about him. Why, it never made no difference to *him*—he'd bet on *any* thing—the dangdest feller. Parson Walker's wife laid very sick once, for a good while, and it seemed as if they warn't going to save her; but one morning he come in, and Smiley up and asked him how she was, and he said she was considerable better—thank the Lord for his inf'nite mercy—and coming on so smart that with the blessing of Prov'dence she'd get well yet; and Smiley, before he thought, says, 'Well, I'll resk two-and-a-half she don't anyway.'

"Thish-yer Smiley had a mare—the boys called her the fifteen-minute nag, but that was only in fun, you know, because of course she was faster than that—and he used to win money on that horse, for all she was so slow and always had the asthma, or the distemper, or the consumption, or something of that kind. They used to give her two or three hundred yards' start, and then pass her under way; but always at the fag end of the race she'd get excited and desperate like, and come cavorting and straddling up, and scattering her legs around limber, sometimes in the air, and sometimes out to one side among the fences, and kicking up m-o-r-e dust and raising m-o-r-e racket with her coughing and sneezing and blowing her nose—and *always* fetch up at the stand just about a neck ahead, as near as you could cipher it down.

"And he had a little small bull-pup, that to look at him you'd think he warn't worth a cent but to set around and look ornery and lay for a chance to steal something. But as soon as money was up on him he was a different dog; his under-jaw'd begin to stick out like the fo'castle of a steamboat, and his teeth would uncover and shine like the furnaces. And a dog might tackle him and bully-rag him, and bite him, and throw him over his shoulder two or three times, and Andrew Jackson—which was the name of the pup—Andrew Jackson would never let on but what *he* was satisfied, and hadn't expected nothing else—and the bets being doubled and doubled on the other side all the time, till the money was all up; and then all of a sudden he would grab that other dog jest by the j'int of his hind leg and freeze to it—not chaw, you understand, but only just grip and hang on till they throwed up the sponge, if it was a year. Smiley always come out winner on that pup, till he harnessed a dog once that didn't have no hind legs, because they'd been sawed off in a circular saw, and when the thing had gone along far enough, and the money was all up, and he come to make a snatch for his pet holt, he see in a minute how he'd been imposed on, and how the other dog had him in the door, so to speak, and he 'peared surprised, and then he looked sorter discouraged-like, and didn't try no more to win the fight, and so he got shucked out bad. He give Smiley a look, as much as to say his heart was broke, and it was *his* fault, for putting up a dog that hadn't no hind legs for him to take holt of, which was his main dependence in a fight, and then he limped off a piece and laid down and died. It was a good pup, was that Andrew Jackson, and would have made a name for hisself if he'd lived, for the stuff was in him and he had genius—I know it, because he hadn't no opportunities to speak of, and it don't stand to reason that a dog could make such a fight as he could under them circumstances if he hadn't no talent. It always makes me feel sorry when I think of that last fight of his'n, and the way it turned out.

"Well, thish-yer Smiley had rat-tarriers, and chicken cocks, and tomcats and all them kind of things, till you couldn't rest, and you couldn't fetch nothing for him to bet on but he'd match you. He ketched a frog one day, and took him home, and said he cal'lated to educate him; and so he never done nothing for three months but set in his back yard and learn that frog to jump. And you bet you he *did* learn him, too. He'd give him a little punch behind, and the next minute you'd see that frog whirling in the air like a doughnut—see him turn one summerset, or maybe a couple, if he got a good start, and come down flat-footed and all right, like a cat. He got him up so in the matter of ketching flies, and kep' him in practice so constant, that he'd nail a fly every time as fur as he could see him. Smiley said all a frog wanted was education, and he could do 'most anything—and I believe him. Why, I've seen him set Dan'l Webster down here on this floor—Dan'l Webster was the name of the frog—and sing out, 'Flies, Dan'l, flies!' and quicker'n you could wink he'd spring straight up and snake a fly off'n the counter there, and flop down on the floor ag'in as solid as a gob of mud, and fall to scratching the side of his head with his hind foot as indifferent as if he hadn't no idea he'd been doin' any more'n any frog might do. You never see a frog so modest and straightfor'ard as he was, for all he was so gifted. And when it come to fair and square jumping on a dead level, he could get over more ground at one strad-dle than any animal of his breed you ever see. Jumping on a dead level was his strong suit, you understand; and when it come to that, Smiley would ante up money on him as long as he had a red. Smiley was monstrous proud of his frog, and well he might be, for fellers that had traveled and been everywheres all said he laid over any frog that ever *they* see.

"Well, Smiley kep' the beast in a little lattice box, and he used to fetch him down-town sometimes and lay for a bet. One day a feller—a stranger in the camp, he was—come acrost him with his box, and says:

" 'What might it be that you've got in the box?'

"And Smiley says, sorter indifferent-like, 'It might be a parrot, or it might be a canary, maybe, but it ain't—it's only just a frog.'

"And the feller took it, and looked at it careful, and turned it round this way and that, and says, 'H'm—so 'tis. Well, what's *he* good for?'

" 'Well,' Smiley says, easy and careless, 'he's good enough for *one* thing, I should judge—he can outjump any frog in Calaveras County.'

"The feller took the box again, and took another long, particular look, and give it back to Smiley, and says, very deliberate, 'Well,' he says, 'I don't see no p'ints about that frog that's any better'n any other frog.'

" 'Maybe you don't,' Smiley says. 'Maybe you understand frogs and maybe you don't understand 'em; maybe you've had experience, and maybe you ain't only a amature, as it were. Anyways, I've got *my* opinion, and I'll resk forty dollars that he can outjump any frog in Calaveras County.'

"And the feller studied a minute, and then says, kinder sad-like, 'Well, I'm only a stranger here, and I ain't got no frog; but if I had a frog, I'd bet you.'

"And then Smiley says, 'That's all right—that's all right—if you'll hold my box a minute, I'll go and get you a frog.' And so the feller took the box, and put up his forty dollars along with Smiley's, and set down to wait.

"So he set there a good while thinking and thinking to himself, and then he got the frog out and prized his mouth open and took a teaspoon and filled him full of quail-shot—filled him pretty near up to his chin—and set him on the floor. Smiley he went to the swamp and slopped around in the mud for a long time, and finally he ketched a frog, and fetched him in, and give him to this feller, and says:

" 'Now, if you're ready, set him alongside of Dan'l, with his fore paws just even with Dan'l's, and I'll give the word.' Then he says, 'One—two—three—*git!*' and him and the feller touched up the frogs from behind, and the new frog hopped off lively, but Dan'l give a heave, and hysted up his shoulders—so—like a Frenchman, but it warn't no use—he couldn't budge; he was planted as solid as a church, and he couldn't no more stir than if he was anchored out. Smiley was a good deal surprised, and he was disgusted too, but he didn't have no idea what the matter was, of course.

"The feller took the money and started away; and when he was going out at the door, he sorter jerked his thumb over his shoulder—so—at Dan'l, and says again, very deliberate, 'Well,' he says, '*I* don't see no p'ints about that frog that's any better'n any other frog.'

"Smiley he stood scratching his head and looking down at Dan'l a long time, and at last he says, 'I do wonder what in the nation that frog throw'd off for—I wonder if there ain't something the matter with him—he 'pears to look mighty baggy, somehow.' And he ketched Dan'l by the nap of the neck, and hefted him, and says, 'Why blame my cats if he don't weigh five pound!' and turned him upside down and he belched out a double handful of shot. And then he see how it was, and he was the maddest man—he set the frog down and took out after that feller, but he never ketched him. And—"

[Here Simon Wheeler heard his name called from the front yard, and got up to see what was wanted.] And turning to me as he moved away, he said: "Just set where you are, stranger, and rest easy—I ain't going to be gone a second."

But, by your leave, I did not think that a continuation of the history of the enterprising vagabond *Jim* Smiley would be likely to afford me much information concerning the Rev. *Leonidas* W. Smiley, and so I started away.

At the door I met the sociable Wheeler returning, and he buttonholed me and recommenced:

"Well, thish-yer Smiley had a yaller one-eyed cow that didn't have no tail, only just a short stump like a bannanner, and—"

However, lacking both time and inclination, I did not wait to hear about the afflicted cow, but took my leave.

Journalism in Tennessee

The editor of the Memphis *Avalanche* swoops thus mildly down upon a correspondent who posted him as a Radical: "While he was writing the first word, the middle word, dotting his i's, crossing his t's, and punching his period, he knew he was concocting a sentence that was saturated with infamy and reeking with falsehood." —*Exchange*.

I WAS told by the physician that a Southern climate would improve my health, and so I went down to Tennessee and got a berth on the *Morning Glory and Johnson County War-Whoop*, as associate editor. When I went on duty I found the chief editor sitting tilted back in a three-legged chair with his feet on a pine table. There was another pine table in the room, and another afflicted chair, and both were half buried under newspapers and scraps and sheets of manuscript. There was a wooden box of sand, sprinkled with cigar stubs and "old soldiers," and a stove with a door hanging by its upper hinge. The chief editor had a long-tailed black cloth frock coat on, and white linen pants. His boots were small and neatly blacked. He wore a ruffled shirt, a large seal ring, a standing collar of obsolete pattern and a checkered neckerchief with the ends hanging down. Date of costume, about 1848. He was smoking a cigar and trying to think of a word. And in trying to think of a word, and in pawing his hair for it, he had rumpled his locks a good deal. He was scowling fearfully, and I judged that he was concocting a particularly knotty editorial. He told me to take the exchanges and skim through them and write up the "Spirit of the Tennessee Press," condensing into the article all of their contents that seemed of interest.

I wrote as follows:

"SPIRIT OF THE TENNESSEE PRESS.

"The editors of the *Semi-Weekly Earthquake* evidently labor under a misapprehension with regard to the Ballyhack railroad. It is not the object of the company to leave Buzzardville off to one side. On the contrary they consider it one of the most important points along the line, and consequently can have no desire to slight it. The gentlemen of the *Earthquake* will of course take pleasure in making the correction.

"John W. Blossom, Esq., the able editor of the Higginsville *Thunderbolt and Battle-Cry of Freedom*, arrived in the city yesterday. He is stopping at the Van Buren House.

"We observe that our cotemporary of the Mud Springs *Morning Howl* has fallen into the error of supposing that the election of Van Werter is not an established fact, but he will have discovered his mistake before this reminder reaches him, no doubt. He was doubtless misled by incomplete election returns.

"It is pleasant to note that the city of Blathersville is endeavoring to contract with some New York gentlemen to pave its well nigh impassable streets with the Nicholson pavement. But it is difficult to accomplish a desire like this since Memphis got some New Yorkers to do a like service for her and then declined to pay for it. However the *Daily Hurrah* still urges the measure with ability, and seems confident of ultimate success.

"We are pained to learn that Col. Bascom, chief editor of the *Dying Shriek for Liberty*, fell in the street a few evenings since and broke his leg. He has lately been suffering with debility, caused by overwork and anxiety on account of sickness in his family, and it is supposed that he fainted from the exertion of walking too much in the sun."

I passed my manuscript over to the chief editor for acceptance, alteration or destruction. He glanced at it and his face clouded. He ran his eye down the pages, and his countenance grew portentous. It was easy to see that something was wrong. Presently he sprang up and said:

"Thunder and lightning! Do you suppose I am going to speak of those cattle that way? Do you suppose my subscribers are going to stand such gruel as that? Give me the pen!"

I never saw a pen scrape and scratch its way so viciously, or plough through another man's verbs and adjectives so relentlessly. While he was in the midst of his work somebody shot at him through the open window and marred the symmetry of his ear.

"Ah," said he, "that is that scoundrel Smith, of the *Moral Volcano*—he was due yesterday." And he snatched a navy revolver from his belt and fired. Smith dropped, shot in the thigh. The shot spoiled Smith's aim, who was just taking a second chance, and he crippled a stranger. It was me. Merely a finger shot off.

Then the chief editor went on with his erasures and interlineations. Just as he finished them a hand-grenade came down the stove-pipe, and the explosion shivered the stove into a thousand fragments. However, it did no further damage, except that a vagrant piece knocked a couple of my teeth out.

"That stove is utterly ruined," said the chief editor.

I said I believed it was.

"Well, no matter—don't want it this kind of weather. I know the man that did it. I'll get him. Now *here* is the way this stuff ought to be written."

I took the manuscript. It was scarred with erasures and interlineations till its mother wouldn't have known it, if it had had one. It now read as follows:

"SPIRIT OF THE TENNESSEE PRESS.

"The inveterate liars of the *Semi-Weekly Earthquake* are evidently endeavoring to palm off upon a noble and chivalrous people another of their vile and brutal falsehoods with regard to that most glorious conception of the nineteenth century, the Ballyhack railroad. The idea that Buzzardville was to be left off at one side originated in their own fulsome brains—or rather in the settlings which *they* regard as brains. They had better swallow this lie, and not stop to chew it, either, if they want to save their abandoned, reptile carcasses the cowhiding they so richly deserve.

"That ass, Blossom of the Higginsville *Thunderbolt and Battle-Cry of Freedom*, is down here again, bumming his board at the Van Buren.

"We observe that the besotted blackguard of the Mud Springs *Morning Howl* is giving out, with his usual propensity for lying, that Van Werter is not elected. The heaven-born mission of journalism is to disseminate truth—to eradicate error—to educate, refine and elevate the tone of public morals and manners, and make all men more gentle, more virtuous, more charitable, and in all ways better, and holier and happier—and yet this black-hearted villain, this hell-spawned miscreant, prostitutes his great office persistently to the dissemination of falsehood, calumny, vituperation and degrading vulgarity. His paper is notoriously unfit to take into the people's homes, and ought to be banished to the gambling hells and brothels where the mass of reeking pollution which does duty as its editor, lives and moves, and has his being.

"Blathersville wants a Nicholson pavement—it wants a jail and a poor-house more. The idea of a pavement in a one-horse town with two gin-mills and a blacksmith shop in it, and that mustard-plaster of a newspaper, the *Daily Hurrah!* Better borrow of Memphis, where the article is cheap. The crawling insect, Buckner, who edits the *Hurrah*, is braying about this pavement business with his customary loud-mouthed imbecility, and imagining that he is talking sense. Such foul, mephitic scum as this verminous Buckner, are a disgrace to journalism.

"That degraded ruffian Bascom, of the *Dying Shriek for Liberty*, fell down and broke his leg yesterday—pity it wasn't his neck. He says it was 'debility caused by overwork and anxiety!' It was debility caused by trying to lug six gallons of forty-rod whisky around town when his hide is only gauged for four, and anxiety about where he was going to bum another six. He 'fainted from the exertion of walking too much in the sun!' And well he might say that—but if he would walk *straight* he would get just as far and not have to walk half as much. For years the pure air of this town has been rendered perilous by the deadly breath of this perambulating pestilence, this pulpy bloat, this steaming, animated tank of mendacity, gin and profanity, this Bascom! Perish all such from out the sacred and majestic mission of journalism!"

"Now *that* is the way to write—peppery and to the point. Mush-and-milk journalism gives me the fan-tods."

About this time a brick came through the window with a splintering crash, and gave me a considerable of a jolt in the middle of the back. I moved out of range—I began to feel in the way. The chief said:

"That was the Colonel, likely, I've been expecting him for two days. He will be up, now, right away."

He was correct. The "Colonel" appeared in the door a moment afterward, with a dragoon revolver in his hand. He said:

"Sir, have I the honor of addressing the white-livered poltroon who edits this mangy sheet?"

"You have—be seated, Sir—be careful of the chair, one of the legs is gone. I believe I have the pleasure of addressing the blatant, black-hearted scoundrel, Col. Blatherskite Tecumseh?"

"The same. I have a little account to settle with you. If you are at leisure, we will begin."

"I have an article on the 'Encouraging Progress of Moral and Intellectual Development in America,' to finish, but there is no hurry. Begin."

Both pistols rang out their fierce clamor at the same instant. The chief lost a lock of hair, and the Colonel's bullet ended its career in the fleshy part of my thigh. The Colonel's left shoulder was clipped a little. They fired again. Both missed their men this time, but I got my share, a shot in the arm. At the third fire both gentlemen were wounded slightly, and I had a knuckle chipped. I then said I believed I would go out and take a walk, as this was a private matter and I had a delicacy about participating in it further. But both gentlemen begged me to keep my seat and assured me that I was not in the way. I had thought differently, up to this time.

They then talked about the elections and the crops a while, and I fell to tying up my wounds. But presently they opened fire again with animation, and every shot took effect—but it is proper to remark that five out of the six fell to my share. The sixth one mortally wounded the Colonel, who remarked, with fine humor, that he would have to say good morning, now, as he had business up town. He then inquired the way to the undertaker's and left. The chief turned to me and said:

"I am expecting company to dinner and shall have to get ready. It will be a favor to me if you will read proof and attend to the customers."

I winced a little at the idea of attending to the customers, but I was too bewildered by the fusillade that was still ringing in my ears to think of anything to say. He continued:

"Jones will be here at 3. Cowhide him. Gillespie will call earlier, perhaps—throw him out of the window. Ferguson will be along about 4—kill him. That is all for to-day, I believe. If you have any odd time, you may write a blistering article on the police—give the Chief Inspector rats. The cowhides are under the table; weapons in the drawer—ammunition there in the corner—lint and bandages up there in the pigeonholes. In case of accident, go to Lancet, the surgeon, down stairs. He advertises—we take it out in trade."

He was gone. I shuddered. At the end of the next three hours I had been through perils so awful that all peace of mind and all cheerfulness had gone from me. Gillespie had called, and thrown *me* out of the window. Jones arrived promptly, and when I got ready to do the cowhiding, he took the job off my hands. In an encounter with a stranger, not in the bill of fare, I had lost my scalp. Another stranger, by the name of Thompson, left me a mere wreck and ruin of chaotic rags. And at last, at bay in the corner, and beset by an infuriated mob of editors, blacklegs, politicians and desperadoes, who raved and swore and flourished their weapons about my head till the air shimmered with glancing flashes of steel, I was in the act of resigning my berth on the paper when the chief arrived, and with him a rabble of charmed and enthusiastic friends. Then ensued a scene of riot and carnage such as no human pen, or steel one either, could describe. People were shot, probed, dismembered, blown up, thrown out of the window. There was a brief tornado of murky blasphemy, with a confused and frantic war-dance glimmering through it, and then all was over. In five minutes there was silence, and the gory chief and I sat alone and surveyed the sanguinary ruin that strewed the floor around us. He said:

"You'll like this place when you get used to it." I said:

"I'll have to get you to excuse me. I think maybe I might write to suit

you, after a while, as soon as I had had some practice and learned
the language—I am confident I could. But to speak the plain truth,
that sort of energy of expression has its inconveniences, and a man is
liable to interruption. You see that, yourself. Vigorous writing is calculated to elevate the public, no doubt, but then I do not like to attract so
much attention as it calls forth. I can't write with comfort when I am
interrupted so much as I have been to-day. I like this berth well enough,
but I don't like to be left here to wait on the customers. The experiences
are novel, I grant you, and entertaining, too, after a fashion, but they are
not judiciously distributed. A gentleman shoots at you, through the window, and cripples *me*; a bomb-shell comes down the stove-pipe for your
gratification, and sends the stove door down *my* throat; a friend drops
in to swap compliments with you, and freckles *me* with bullet holes till
my skin won't hold my principles; you go to dinner, and Jones comes
with his cowhide, Gillespie throws me out of the window, Thompson
tears all my clothes off, and an entire stranger takes my scalp with the
easy freedom of an old acquaintance; and in less than five minutes all
the blackguards in the country arrive in their war paint and proceed to
scare the rest of me to death with their tomahawks. Take it altogether, I
never have had such a spirited time in all my life as I have had to-day.
No. I like you, and I like your calm, unruffled way of explaining things
to the customers, but you see I am not used to it. The Southern heart
is too impulsive—Southern hospitality is too lavish with the stranger.
The paragraphs which I have written to-day, and into whose cold sen-
tences your masterly hand has infused the fervent spirit of Tennesseean
journalism, will wake up another nest of hornets. All that mob of editors will come—and they will come hungry, too, and want somebody
for breakfast. I shall have to bid you adieu. I decline to be present at
these festivities. I came South for my health—I will go back on the same
errand, and suddenly. Tennessee journalism is too stirring for me." After which, we parted, with mutual regret, and I took apartments at the
hospital.

About Barbers

ALL THINGS CHANGE except barbers, the ways of barbers, and the surroundings of barbers. These never change. What one experiences in a barber shop the first time he enters one, is what he always experiences in barber shops afterward till the end of his days. I got shaved this morning as usual. A man approached the door from Jones street as I approached it from Main—a thing that always happens. I hurried up, but it was of no use; he entered the door one little step ahead of me, and I followed in on his heels and saw him take the only vacant chair, the one presided over by the best barber. It always happens so. I sat down, hoping that I might fall heir to the chair belonging to the better of the remaining two barbers, for he had already begun combing his man's hair, while his comrade was not yet quite done rubbing up and oiling his customer's locks. I watched the probabilities with strong interest. When I saw that No. 2 was gaining on No. 1, my interest grew to solicitude. When No. 1 stopped a moment to make change on a bath ticket for a new-comer, and lost ground in the race, my solicitude rose to anxiety. When No. 1 caught up again, and both he and his comrade were pulling the towels away and brushing the powder from their customers' cheeks, and it was about an even thing which one would say "Next!" first, my very breath stood still with the suspense. But when, at the final culminating moment, No. 1 stopped to pass a comb a couple of times through his customer's eyebrows, I saw that he had lost the race by a single instant, and I rose indignant and quitted the shop, to keep from falling into the hands of No. 2; for I have none of that enviable firmness that enables a man to look calmly into the eyes of a waiting barber and tell him he will wait for his fellow-barber's chair. I stayed out fifteen minutes, and then went back, hoping for better luck. Of course all the chairs were occupied now, and four men sat waiting, silent, unsociable, distraught, and looking bored, as men always do who are awaiting their turn in a barber's shop. I sat down in one of the iron-armed compartments of an old sofa, and put in the time for a while, reading the framed advertisements of all sorts of quack nostrums for dyeing and coloring the hair. Then I read the greasy names on the private bay rum bottles; read the names and noted the numbers on the private shaving cups in the pigeon-holes; studied the stained and damaged cheap prints on the walls, of battles, early Presidents, and voluptuous, recumbent sultanas, and the tiresome and everlasting young girl putting her grandfather's spectacles on; execrated in my heart the cheerful canary and the distracting parrot that few barber shops are without. Finally, I searched out the least dilapidated of the last year's illustrated papers that littered the foul centre-table, and conned their unjustifiable misrepresentations of old forgotten events. At last my turn came. A voice said "Next!" and I surrendered to—No. 2 of course. It always happens so. I said meekly that I was in a hurry, and it affected him as strongly as if he had never heard it. He shoved up my head and put a napkin under it. He ploughed his fingers into my collar and fixed a towel there. He explored my hair with his claws and suggested that it needed trimming. I said I did not want it trimmed. He explored again and said it was pretty long for the present style—better have a little taken off; it needed it behind, especially. I said I had had it cut only a week before. He yearned over it reflectively a moment, and then asked, with a disparaging manner, who cut it. I came back at him promptly with a "You did!" I had him there. Then he fell to stirring up his lather and regarding himself in the glass, stopping now and then to get close and examine his chin critically or torture a pimple. Then he lathered one side of my face thoroughly, and was about to lather the other, when a dog fight attracted his attention, and he ran to the window and stayed and saw it out, losing two shillings on the result in bets with the other barbers, a thing which gave me great satisfaction. He finished lathering, meantime getting the brush into my mouth only twice, and then began to rub in the suds with his hand; and as he now had his head turned, discussing the dog fight with the other barbers, he naturally shovelled considerable lather into my mouth without knowing it, but I did. He now began to sharpen his razor on an old suspender, and was delayed a good deal on account of a controversy about a cheap masquerade ball he had figured at the night before, in red cambric and bogus ermine, as some kind of a king. He was so gratified with being chaffed about some damsel whom he had smitten with his charms, that he used every means to continue the controversy by pretending to be annoyed at the chaffings of his fellows. This matter begot more surveyings of himself in the glass, and he put down his razor and brushed his hair with elaborate care, plastering an inverted arch of it down on his forehead, accomplishing an accurate "part" behind, and brushing the two wings forward over his ears with nice exactness. In the mean time the lather was drying on my face, and apparently eating into my vitals. Now he began to shave, digging his fingers into my countenance to stretch the skin, making a handle of my nose now and then, bundling and tumbling my head this way and that as convenience in shaving demanded, and "hawking" and expectorating pleasantly all the while. As long as he was on the tough sides of my face I did not suffer; but when he began to rake, and rip, and tug at my chin, the tears came. I did not mind his getting so close down to me; I did not mind his garlic, because all barbers eat garlic, I suppose; but there was an added something that made me fear that he was decaying inwardly while still alive, and this gave me much concern. He now put his finger into my mouth to assist him in shaving the corners of my upper lip, and it was by this bit of circumstantial evidence that I discovered that a part of his duties in the shop was to clean the kerosene lamps. I had often wondered in an indolent way whether the barbers did that, or whether it was the boss. About this time I was amusing myself trying to guess where he would be most likely to cut me this time, but he got ahead of me and sliced me on the end of the chin before I had got my mind made up. He immediately sharpened his razor—he might have done it before. I do not like a close shave, and would not let him go over me a second time. I tried to get him to put up his razor, dreading that he would make for the side of my chin, my pet tender spot, a place which a razor cannot touch twice without making trouble. But he said he only wanted to just smooth off one little roughness, and in that same moment he slipped his razor along the forbidden ground, and the dreaded pimple-signs of a close shave rose up smarting and answered to the call. Now he soaked his towel in bay rum, and slapped it all over my face nastily; slapped it over as if a human being ever yet washed his face in that way. Then he dried it by slapping with the dry part of the towel, as if a human being ever dried his face in such a fashion; but a barber seldom rubs you like a Christian. Next he poked bay rum into the cut place with his towel, then choked the wound with powdered starch, then soaked it with bay rum again, and would have gone on soaking and powdering it for evermore, no doubt, if I had not rebelled and begged off. He powdered my whole face now, straightened me up and began to plough my hair thoughtfully with his hands and examine his fingers critically. Then he suggested a shampoo, and said my hair needed it badly, very badly. I observed that I had shampooed it myself very thoroughly in the bath yesterday. I "had him" again. He next recommended some of "Smith's Hair Glorifier," and offered to sell me a bottle. I declined. He praised the new perfume, "Jones's Delight of the Toilet," and proposed to sell me some of that. I declined again. He tendered me a tooth-wash atrocity of his own invention, and when I declined, offered to trade knives with me. He returned to business after the miscarriage of this last enterprise, sprinkled me all over, legs and all, greased my hair in defiance of my protests against it, rubbed and scrubbed a good deal of it out by the roots, and combed and brushed the rest, parting it behind and plastering the eternal inverted arch of hair down on my forehead, and then, while combing my scant eyebrows and defiling them with pomade, strung out an account of the achievements of a six-ounce black and tan terrier of his till I heard the whistles blow for noon, and knew I was five minutes too late for the train. Then he snatched away the towel, brushed it lightly about my face, passed his comb through my eyebrows once more, and gayly sang out "Next!"

This barber fell down and died of apoplexy two hours later. I am waiting over a day for my revenge—I am going to attend his funeral.

A Literary Nightmare

WILL THE READER please to cast his eye over the following verses, and see if he can discover anything harmful in them?

> "Conductor, when you receive a fare,
>   Punch in the presence of the passenjare!
>   A blue trip slip for an eight-cent fare,
>   A buff trip slip for a six-cent fare,
>   A pink trip slip for a three-cent fare,
>   Punch in the presence of the passenjare!
>   CHORUS.
>   Punch, brothers! punch with care!
>   Punch in the presence of the passenjare!"

I came across these jingling rhymes in a newspaper, a little while ago, and read them a couple of times. They took instant and entire possession of me. All through breakfast they went waltzing through my brain; and when, at last, I rolled up my napkin, I could not tell whether I had eaten anything or not. I had carefully laid out my day's work the day before—a thrilling tragedy in the novel which I am writing. I went to my den to begin my deed of blood. I took up my pen, but all I could get it to say was, "Punch in the presence of the passenjare." I fought hard for an hour, but it was useless. My head kept humming, "A blue trip slip for an eight-cent fare, a buff trip slip for a six-cent fare," and so on and so on, without peace or respite. The day's work was ruined—I could see that plainly enough. I gave up and drifted down town, and presently discovered that my feet were keeping time to that relentless jingle. When I could stand it no longer I altered my step. But it did no good; those rhymes accommodated themselves to the new step and went on harassing me just as before. I returned home, and suffered all the afternoon; suffered all through an unconscious and unrefreshing dinner; suffered, and cried, and jingled all through the evening; went to bed and rolled, tossed, and jingled right along, the same as ever; got up at midnight frantic, and tried to read; but there was nothing visible upon the whirling page except "Punch! punch in the presence of the passenjare." By sunrise I was out of my mind, and everybody marveled and was distressed at the idiotic burden of my ravings,—"Punch! oh, punch! punch in the presence of the passenjare!"

Two days later, on Saturday morning, I arose, a tottering wreck, and went forth to fulfill an engagement with a valued friend, the Rev. Mr. —— , to walk to the Talcott Tower, ten miles distant. He stared at me, but asked no questions. We started. Mr. —— talked, talked, talked—as is his wont. I said nothing; I heard nothing. At the end of a mile, Mr. —— said,—

"Mark, are you sick? I never saw a man look so haggard and worn and absent-minded. Say something; do!"

Drearily, without enthusiasm, I said: "Punch, brothers, punch with care! Punch in the presence of the passenjare!"

My friend eyed me blankly, looked perplexed, then said,—

"I do not think I get your drift, Mark. There does not seem to be any relevancy in what you have said, certainly nothing sad; and yet—maybe it was the way you *said* the words—I never heard anything that sounded so pathetic. What is"—

But I heard no more. I was already far away with my pitiless, heart-breaking "blue trip slip for an eight-cent fare, buff trip slip for a six-cent fare, pink trip slip for a three-cent fare; punch in the presence of the passenjare." I do not know what occurred during the other nine miles. However, all of a sudden Mr. —— laid his hand on my shoulder and shouted,—

"Oh, wake up! wake up! wake up! Don't sleep all day! Here we are at the Tower, man! I have talked myself deaf and dumb and blind, and never got a response. Just look at this magnificent autumn landscape! Look at it! look at it! Feast your eyes on it! You have traveled; you have seen boasted landscapes elsewhere. Come, now, deliver an honest opinion. What do you say to this?"

I sighed wearily, and murmured,—

"A buff trip slip for a six-cent fare, a pink trip slip for a three-cent fare, punch in the presence of the passenjare."

Rev. Mr. —— stood there, very grave, full of concern, apparently, and looked long at me; then he said,—

"Mark, there is something about this that I cannot understand. Those are about the same words you said before; there does not seem to be anything in them, and yet they nearly break my heart when you say them. Punch in the—how is it they go?"

I began at the beginning and repeated all the lines. My friend's face lighted with interest. He said,—

"Why, what a captivating jingle it is! It is almost music. It flows along so nicely. I have nearly caught the rhymes myself. Say them over just once more, and then I'll have them, sure."

I said them over. Then Mr. —— said them. He made one little mistake, which I corrected. The next time and the next he got them right. Now a great burden seemed to tumble from my shoulders. That torturing jingle departed out of my brain, and a grateful sense of rest and peace descended upon me. I was light-hearted enough to sing; and I did sing for half an hour, straight along, as we went jogging homeward. Then my freed tongue found blessed speech again, and the pent talk of many a weary hour began to gush and flow. It flowed on and on, joyously, jubilantly, until the fountain was empty and dry. As I wrung my friend's hand at parting, I said,—

"Have n't we had a royal good time! But now I remember, you

have n't said a word for two hours. Come, come, out with something!"

The Rev. Mr. —— turned a lacklustre eye upon me, drew a deep sigh, and said, without animation, without apparent consciousness,—

"Punch, brothers, punch with care! Punch in the presence of the passenjare!"

A pang shot through me as I said to myself, "Poor fellow, poor fellow! *he* has got it, now."

I did not see Mr. —— for two or three days after that. Then, on Tuesday evening, he staggered into my presence and sank dejectedly into a seat. He was pale, worn; he was a wreck. He lifted his faded eyes to my face and said,—

"Ah, Mark, it was a ruinous investment that I made in those heartless rhymes. They have ridden me like a nightmare, day and night, hour after hour, to this very moment. Since I saw you I have suffered the torments of the lost. Saturday evening I had a sudden call, by telegraph, and took the night train for Boston. The occasion was the death of a valued old friend who had requested that I should preach his funeral sermon. I took my seat in the cars and set myself to framing the discourse. But I never got beyond the opening paragraph; for then the train started and the car-wheels began their 'clack-clack-clack-clack! clack-clack-clack-clack!' and right away those odious rhymes fitted themselves to that accompaniment. For an hour I sat there and set a syllable of those rhymes to every separate and distinct clack the car-wheels made. Why, I was as fagged out, then, as if I had been chopping wood all day. My skull was splitting with headache. It seemed to me that I must go mad if I sat there any longer; so I undressed and went to bed. I stretched myself out in my berth, and—well, you know what the result was. The thing went right along, just the same. 'Clack-clack-clack, a blue trip slip, clack-clack-clack, for an eight-cent fare; clack-clack-clack, a buff trip slip, clack-clack-clack, for a six-cent fare, and so on, and so on, and so on—*punch*, in the presence of the passenjare!' Sleep? Not a single wink! I was almost a lunatic when I got to Boston. Don't ask me about the funeral. I did the best I could, but every solemn individual sentence was meshed and tangled and woven in and out with 'Punch, brothers, punch with care, punch in the presence of the passenjare.' And the most distressing thing was that my *delivery* dropped into the undulating rhythm of those pulsing rhymes, and I could actually catch absent-minded people nodding *time* to the swing of it with their stupid heads. And, Mark, you may believe it or not, but before I got through, the entire assemblage were placidly bobbing their heads in solemn unison, mourners, undertaker, and all. The moment I had finished, I fled to the anteroom in a state bordering on frenzy. Of course it would be my luck to find a sorrowing and aged maiden aunt of the deceased there, who had arrived from Springfield too late to get into the church. She began to sob, and said,—

" 'Oh, oh, he is gone, he is gone, and I did n't see him before he died!'

" 'Yes!' I said, 'he *is* gone, he *is* gone, he *is* gone—oh, *will* this suffering never cease!'

" '*You* loved him, then! Oh, you too loved him!'

" 'Loved him! Loved *who?*'

" 'Why, my poor George! my poor nephew!'

" 'Oh—*him!* Yes—oh, yes, yes. Certainly—certainly. Punch—punch—oh, this misery will kill me!'

" 'Bless you! bless you, sir, for these sweet words! *I*, too, suffer in this dear loss. Were you present during his last moments?'

" 'Yes! I—*whose* last moments?'

" '*His*. The dear departed's.'

" 'Yes! Oh, yes—yes—*yes!* I suppose so, I think so, *I* don't know! Oh, certainly—I was there—*I* was there!'

" 'Oh, what a privilege! what a precious privilege! And his last words—oh, tell me, tell me his last words! What did he say?'

" 'He said—he said—oh, my head, my head, my head! He said—he said—he never said *any*thing but Punch, punch, *punch* in the presence of the passenjare! Oh, leave me, madam! In the name of all that is generous, leave me to my madness, my misery, my despair!—a buff trip slip for a six-cent fare, a pink trip slip for a three-cent fare—endu-rance *can* no fur-ther go!—PUNCH in the presence of the passenjare!' "

My friend's hopeless eyes rested upon mine a pregnant minute, and then he said impressively,—

"Mark, you do not say anything. You do not offer me any hope. But, ah me, it is just as well—it is just as well. You could not do me any good. The time has long gone by when words could comfort me. Something tells me that my tongue is doomed to wag forever to the jigger of that remorseless jingle. There—there it is coming on me again: a blue trip slip for an eight-cent fare, a buff trip slip for a"—

Thus murmuring faint and fainter, my friend sank into a peaceful trance and forgot his sufferings in a blessed respite.

How did I finally save him from the asylum? I took him to a neighboring university and made him discharge the burden of his persecuting rhymes into the eager ears of the poor, unthinking students. How is it with *them*, now? The result is too sad to tell. Why did I write this article? It was for a worthy, even a noble, purpose. It was to warn you, reader, if you should come across those merciless rhymes, to avoid them—avoid them as you would a pestilence!

The Stolen White Elephant*

I.

THE FOLLOWING curious history was related to me by a chance railway acquaintance. He was a gentleman more than seventy years of age, and his thoroughly good and gentle face and earnest and sincere manner imprinted the unmistakable stamp of truth upon every statement which fell from his lips. He said:—

You know in what reverence the royal white elephant of Siam is held by the people of that country. You know it is sacred to kings, only kings may possess it, and that it is indeed in a measure even superior to kings, since it receives not merely honor but worship. Very well; five years ago, when the troubles concerning the frontier line arose between Great Britain and Siam, it was presently manifest that Siam had been in the

---

* Left out of "A Tramp Abroad," because it was feared that some of the particulars had been exaggerated, and that others were not true. Before these suspicions had been proven groundless, the book had gone to press. — M. T.

wrong. Therefore every reparation was quickly made, and the British representative stated that he was satisfied and the past should be forgotten. This greatly relieved the King of Siam, and partly as a token of gratitude, but partly also, perhaps, to wipe out any little remaining vestige of unpleasantness which England might feel toward him, he wished to send the Queen a present,—the sole sure way of propitiating an enemy, according to Oriental ideas. This present ought not only to be a royal one, but transcendently royal. Wherefore, what offering could be so meet as that of a white elephant? My position in the Indian civil service was such that I was deemed peculiarly worthy of the honor of conveying the present to her Majesty. A ship was fitted out for me and my servants and the officers and attendants of the elephant, and in due time I arrived in New York harbor and placed my royal charge in admirable quarters in Jersey City. It was necessary to remain awhile in order to recruit the animal's health before resuming the voyage.

All went well during a fortnight,—then my calamities began. The white elephant was stolen! I was called up at dead of night and informed of this fearful misfortune. For some moments I was beside myself with terror and anxiety; I was helpless. Then I grew calmer and collected my faculties. I soon saw my course,—for indeed there was but the one course for an intelligent man to pursue. Late as it was, I flew to New York and got a policeman to conduct me to the headquarters of the detective force. Fortunately I arrived in time, though the chief of the force, the celebrated Inspector Blunt, was just on the point of leaving for his home. He was a man of middle size and compact frame, and when he was thinking deeply he had a way of knitting his brows and tapping his forehead reflectively with his finger, which impressed you at once with the conviction that you stood in the presence of a person of no common order. The very sight of him gave me confidence and made me hopeful. I stated my errand. It did not flurry him in the least; it had no more visible effect upon his iron self-possession than if I had told him somebody had stolen my dog. He motioned me to a seat, and said calmly,—

"Allow me to think a moment, please."

So saying, he sat down at his office table and leaned his head upon his hand. Several clerks were at work at the other end of the room; the scratching of their pens was all the sound I heard during the next six or seven minutes. Meantime the inspector sat there, buried in thought. Finally he raised his head, and there was that in the firm lines of his face which showed me that his brain had done its work and his plan was made. Said he,—and his voice was low and impressive,—

"This is no ordinary case. Every step must be warily taken; each step must be made sure before the next is ventured. And secrecy must be observed,—secrecy profound and absolute. Speak to no one about the matter, not even the reporters. I will take care of *them*; I will see that they get only what it may suit my ends to let them know." He touched a bell; a youth appeared. "Alaric, tell the reporters to remain for the present." The boy retired. "Now let us proceed to business,—and systematically. Nothing can be accomplished in this trade of mine without strict and minute method."

He took a pen and some paper. "Now—name of the elephant?"

"Hassan Ben Ali Ben Selim Abdallah Mohammed Moisé Alhammal Jamsetjejeebhoy Dhuleep Sultan Ebu Bhudpoor."

"Very well. Given name?"

"Jumbo."

"Very well. Place of birth?"

"The capital city of Siam."

"Parents living?"

"No,—dead."

"Had they any other issue besides this one?"

"None. He was an only child."

"Very well. These matters are sufficient under that head. Now please describe the elephant, and leave out no particular, however insignificant,—that is, insignificant from *your* point of view. To men in my profession there *are* no insignificant particulars; they do not exist."

I described,—he wrote. When I was done, he said,—

"Now listen. If I have made any mistakes, correct me."

He read as follows:—

"Height, 19 feet; length from apex of forehead to insertion of tail, 26 feet; length of trunk, 16 feet; length of tail, 6 feet; total length, including trunk and tail, 48 feet; length of tusks, 9½ feet; ears in keeping with these dimensions; footprint resembles the mark left when one up-ends a barrel in the snow; color of the elephant, a dull white; has a hole the size of a plate in each ear for the insertion of jewelry, and possesses the habit in a remarkable degree of squirting water upon spectators and of maltreating with his trunk not only such persons as he is acquainted with, but even entire strangers; limps slightly with his right hind leg, and has a small scar in his left armpit caused by a former boil; had on, when stolen, a castle containing seats for fifteen persons, and a gold-cloth saddle-blanket the size of an ordinary carpet."

There were no mistakes. The inspector touched the bell, handed the description to Alaric, and said,—

"Have fifty thousand copies of this printed at once and mailed to every detective office and pawnbroker's shop on the continent." Alaric retired. "There,—so far, so good. Next, I must have a photograph of the property."

I gave him one. He examined it critically, and said,—

"It must do, since we can do no better; but he has his trunk curled up and tucked into his mouth. That is unfortunate, and is calculated to mislead, for of course he does not usually have it in that position." He touched his bell.

"Alaric, have fifty thousand copies of this photograph made, the first thing in the morning, and mail them with the descriptive circulars."

Alaric retired to execute his orders. The inspector said,—

"It will be necessary to offer a reward, of course. Now as to the amount?"

"What sum would you suggest?"

"To *begin* with, I should say,—well, twenty-five thousand dollars. It is an intricate and difficult business; there are a thousand avenues of escape and opportunities of concealment. These thieves have friends and pals everywhere —"

"Bless me, do you know who they are?"

The wary face, practised in concealing the thoughts and feelings within, gave me no token, nor yet the replying words, so quietly uttered:—

"Never mind about that. I may, and I may not. We generally gather a pretty shrewd inkling of who our man is by the manner of his work and the size of the game he goes after. We are not dealing with a pickpocket or a hall thief, now, make up your mind to that. This property was not 'lifted' by a novice. But, as I was saying, considering the amount of travel which will have to be done, and the diligence with which the thieves will cover up their traces as they move along, twenty-five thousand may be too small a sum to offer, yet I think it worth while to start with that."

So we determined upon that figure, as a beginning. Then this man, whom nothing escaped which could by any possibility be made to serve as a clew, said:—

"There are cases in detective history to show that criminals have been detected through peculiarities in their appetites. Now, what does this elephant eat, and how much?"

"Well, as to *what* he eats,—he will eat *anything*. He will eat a man, he will eat a Bible,—he will eat anything *between* a man and a Bible."

"Good,—very good indeed, but too general. Details are necessary,—details are the only valuable things in our trade. Very well,—as to men. At one meal,—or, if you prefer, during one day,—how many men will he eat, if fresh?"

"He would not care whether they were fresh or not; at a single meal he would eat five ordinary men."

"Very good; five men; we will put that down. What nationalities would he prefer?"

"He is indifferent about nationalities. He prefers acquaintances, but is not prejudiced against strangers."

"Very good. Now, as to Bibles. How many Bibles would he eat at a meal?"

"He would eat an entire edition."

"It is hardly succinct enough. Do you mean the ordinary octavo, or the family illustrated?"

"I think he would be indifferent to illustrations; that is, I think he would not value illustrations above simple letter-press."

"No, you do not get my idea. I refer to bulk. The ordinary octavo Bible weighs about two pounds and a half, while the great quarto with the illustrations weighs ten or twelve. How many Doré Bibles would he eat at a meal?"

"If you knew this elephant, you could not ask. He would take what they had."

"Well, put it in dollars and cents, then. We must get at it somehow. The Doré costs a hundred dollars a copy, Russia leather, bevelled."

"He would require about fifty thousand dollars' worth,—say an edition of five hundred copies."

"Now that is more exact. I will put that down. Very well; he likes men and Bibles; so far, so good. What else will he eat? I want particulars."

"He will leave Bibles to eat bricks, he will leave bricks to eat bottles, he will leave bottles to eat clothing, he will leave clothing to eat cats, he will leave cats to eat oysters, he will leave oysters to eat ham, he will leave ham to eat sugar, he will leave sugar to eat pie, he will leave pie to eat potatoes, he will leave potatoes to eat bran, he will leave bran to eat hay, he will leave hay to eat oats, he will leave oats to eat rice, for he was mainly raised on it. There is nothing whatever that he will not eat but European butter, and he would eat that if he could taste it."

"Very good. General quantity at a meal,—say about—"

"Well, anywhere from a quarter to half a ton."

"And he drinks—"

"Everything that is fluid. Milk, water, whiskey, molasses, castor oil, camphene, carbolic acid,—it is no use to go into particulars; whatever fluid occurs to you set it down. He will drink anything that is fluid, except European coffee."

"Very good. As to quantity?"

"Put it down five to fifteen barrels,—his thirst varies; his other appetites do not."

"These things are unusual. They ought to furnish quite good clews toward tracing him."

He touched the bell.

"Alaric, summon Captain Burns."

Burns appeared. Inspector Blunt unfolded the whole matter to him, detail by detail. Then he said in the clear, decisive tones of a man whose plans are clearly defined in his head, and who is accustomed to command,—

"Captain Burns, detail Detectives Jones, Davis, Halsey, Bates, and Hackett to shadow the elephant."

"Yes, sir."

"Detail Detectives Moses, Dakin, Murphy, Rogers, Tupper, Higgins, and Bartholomew to shadow the thieves."

"Yes, sir."

"Place a strong guard—a guard of thirty picked men, with a relief of thirty—over the place from whence the elephant was stolen, to keep strict watch there night and day, and allow none to approach—except reporters—without written authority from me."

"Yes, sir."

"Place detectives in plain clothes in the railway, steamship, and ferry depots, and upon all roadways leading out of Jersey City, with orders to search all suspicious persons."

"Yes, sir."

"Furnish all these men with photograph and accompanying description of the elephant, and instruct them to search all trains and outgoing ferry-boats and other vessels."

"Yes, sir."

"If the elephant should be found, let him be seized, and the information forwarded to me by telegraph."

"Yes, sir."

"Let me be informed at once if any clews should be found,—footprints of the animal, or anything of that kind."

"Yes, sir."

"Get an order commanding the harbor police to patrol the frontages vigilantly."

"Yes, sir."

"Despatch detectives in plain clothes over all the railways, north as far as Canada, west as far as Ohio, south as far as Washington."

"Yes, sir."

"Place experts in all the telegraph offices to listen to all messages; and let them require that all cipher despatches be interpreted to them."

"Yes, sir."

"Let all these things be done with the utmost secrecy,—mind, the most impenetrable secrecy."

"Yes, sir."

"Report to me promptly at the usual hour."

"Yes, sir."

"Go!"

"Yes, sir."

He was gone.

Inspector Blunt was silent and thoughtful a moment, while the fire in his eye cooled down and faded out. Then he turned to me and said in a placid voice,—

"I am not given to boasting, it is not my habit; but—we shall find the elephant."

I shook him warmly by the hand and thanked him; and I *felt* my thanks, too. The more I had seen of the man the more I liked him, and the more I admired him and marvelled over the mysterious wonders of his profession. Then we parted for the night, and I went home with a far happier heart than I had carried with me to his office.

II.

Next morning it was all in the newspapers, in the minutest detail. It even had additions,—consisting of Detective This, Detective That, and Detective The Other's "Theory" as to how the robbery was done, who the robbers were, and whither they had flown with their booty. There were eleven of these theories, and they covered all the possibilities; and this single fact shows what independent thinkers detectives are. No two theories were alike, or even much resembled each other, save in one striking particular, and in that one all the eleven theories were absolutely agreed. That was, that although the rear of my building was torn out and the only door remained locked, the elephant had not been removed through the rent, but by some other (undiscovered) outlet. All agreed that the robbers had made that rent only to mislead the detectives. That never would have occurred to me or to any other layman, perhaps, but it had not deceived the detectives for a moment. Thus, what I had supposed was the only thing that had no mystery about it was in fact the very thing I had gone furthest astray in. The eleven theories all named the supposed robbers, but no two named the same robbers; the total number of suspected persons was thirty-seven. The various newspaper accounts all closed with the most important opinion of all,—that of Chief Inspector Blunt. A portion of this statement read as follows:—

"The chief knows who the two principals are, namely, 'Brick' Duffy and 'Red' McFadden. Ten days before the robbery was achieved he was already aware that it was to be attempted, and had quietly proceeded to shadow these two noted villains; but unfortunately on the night in question their track was lost, and before it could be found again the bird was flown,—that is, the elephant.

"Duffy and McFadden are the boldest scoundrels in the profession; the chief has reasons for believing that they are the men who stole the stove out of the detective headquarters on a bitter night last winter,—in consequence of which the chief and every detective present were in the hands of the physicians before morning, some with frozen feet, others with frozen fingers, ears, and other members."

When I read the first half of that I was more astonished than ever at the wonderful sagacity of this strange man. He not only saw everything in the present with a clear eye, but even the future could not be hidden from him. I was soon at his office, and said I could not help wishing he had had those men arrested, and so prevented the trouble and loss; but his reply was simple and unanswerable:—

"It is not our province to prevent crime, but to punish it. We cannot punish it until it is committed."

I remarked that the secrecy with which we had begun had been marred by the newspapers; not only all our facts but all our plans and purposes had been revealed; even all the suspected persons had been named; these would doubtless disguise themselves now, or go into hiding.

"Let them. They will find that when I am ready for them my hand will descend upon them, in their secret places, as unerringly as the hand of fate. As to the newspapers, we *must* keep in with them. Fame, reputation, constant public mention,—these are the detective's bread and butter. He must publish his facts, else he will be supposed to have none; he must publish his theory, for nothing is so strange or striking as a detective's theory, or brings him so much wondering respect; we must publish our plans, for these the journals insist upon having, and we could not deny them without offending. We must constantly show the public what we are doing, or they will believe we are doing nothing. It is much pleasanter to have a newspaper say, 'Inspector Blunt's ingenious and extraordinary theory is as follows,' than to have it say some harsh thing, or, worse still, some sarcastic one."

"I see the force of what you say. But I noticed that in one part of your remarks in the papers this morning you refused to reveal your opinion upon a certain minor point."

"Yes, we always do that; it has a good effect. Besides, I had not formed any opinion on that point, any way."

I deposited a considerable sum of money with the inspector, to meet current expenses, and sat down to wait for news. We were expecting the telegrams to begin to arrive at any moment now. Meantime I reread the newspapers and also our descriptive circular, and observed that our $25,000 reward seemed to be offered only to detectives. I said I thought it ought to be offered to anybody who would catch the elephant. The inspector said:—

"It is the detectives who will find the elephant, hence the reward will go to the right place. If other people found the animal, it would only be by watching the detectives and taking advantage of clews and indications stolen from them, and that would entitle the detectives to the reward, after all. The proper office of a reward is to stimulate the men who deliver up their time and their trained sagacities to this sort of work, and not to confer benefits upon chance citizens who stumble upon a capture without having earned the benefits by their own merits and labors."

This was reasonable enough, certainly. Now the telegraphic machine in the corner began to click, and the following despatch was the result:—

FLOWER STATION, N. Y., 7.30 A. M.
Have got a clew. Found a succession of deep tracks across a farm near here. Followed them two miles east without result; think elephant went west. Shall now shadow him in that direction.

DARLEY, *Detective*.

"Darley's one of the best men on the force," said the inspector. "We shall hear from him again before long."
Telegram No. 2 came:—

BARKER'S, N. J., 7.40 A. M.
Just arrived. Glass factory broken open here during night, and eight hundred bottles taken. Only water in large quantity near here is five miles distant. Shall strike for there. Elephant will be thirsty. Bottles were empty.

BAKER, *Detective*.

"That promises well, too," said the inspector. "I told you the creature's appetites would not be bad clews."
Telegram No. 3:—

TAYLORVILLE, L. I., 8.15 A. M.

A haystack near here disappeared during night. Probably eaten. Have got a clew, and am off.

HUBBARD, *Detective*.

"How he does move around!" said the inspector. "I knew we had a difficult job on hand, but we shall catch him yet."

FLOWER STATION, N. Y., 9 A. M.

Shadowed the tracks three miles westward. Large, deep, and ragged. Have just met a farmer who says they are not elephant tracks. Says they are holes where he dug up saplings for shade-trees when ground was frozen last winter. Give me orders how to proceed.

DARLEY, *Detective*.

"Aha! a confederate of the thieves! The thing grows warm," said the inspector.

He dictated the following telegram to Darley:—

Arrest the man and force him to name his pals. Continue to follow the tracks,—to the Pacific, if necessary.

Chief BLUNT.

Next telegram:—

CONEY POINT, PA., 8.45 A. M.

Gas office broken open here during night and three months' unpaid gas bills taken. Have got a clew and am away.

MURPHY, *Detective*.

"Heavens!" said the inspector; "would he eat gas bills?"

"Through ignorance,—yes; but they cannot support life. At least, unassisted."

Now came this exciting telegram:—

IRONVILLE, N. Y., 9.30 A. M.

Just arrived. This village in consternation. Elephant passed through here at five this morning. Some say he went east, some say west, some north, some south,—but all say they did not wait to notice particularly. He killed a horse; have secured a piece of it for a clew. Killed it with his trunk; from style of blow, think he struck it left-handed. From position in which horse lies, think elephant travelled northward along line of Berkley railway. Has four and a half hours' start, but I move on his track at once.

HAWES, *Detective*.

I uttered exclamations of joy. The inspector was as self-contained as a graven image. He calmly touched his bell.

"Alaric, send Captain Burns here."

Burns appeared.

"How many men are ready for instant orders?"

"Ninety-six, sir."

"Send them north at once. Let them concentrate along the line of the Berkley road north of Ironville."

"Yes, sir."

"Let them conduct their movements with the utmost secrecy. As fast as others are at liberty, hold them for orders."

"Yes, sir."

"Go!"

"Yes, sir."

Presently came another telegram:—

> SAGE CORNERS, N. Y., 10.30.
> Just arrived. Elephant passed through here at 8.15. All escaped from the town but a policeman. Apparently elephant did not strike at policeman, but at the lamp-post. Got both. I have secured a portion of the policeman as clew.
> STUMM, *Detective.*

"So the elephant has turned westward," said the inspector. "However, he will not escape, for my men are scattered all over that region."

The next telegram said:—

> GLOVER'S, 11.15.
> Just arrived. Village deserted, except sick and aged. Elephant passed through three quarters of an hour ago. The anti-temperance mass meeting was in session; he put his trunk in at a window and washed it out with water from cistern. Some swallowed it—since dead; several drowned. Detectives Cross and O'Shaughnessy were passing through town, but going south,—so missed elephant. Whole region for many miles around in terror,—people flying from their homes. Wherever they turn they meet elephant, and many are killed.
> BRANT, *Detective.*

I could have shed tears, this havoc so distressed me. But the inspector only said,—

"You see,—we are closing in on him. He feels our presence; he has turned eastward again."

Yet further troublous news was in store for us. The telegraph brought this: —

HOGANPORT, 12.19.

Just arrived. Elephant passed through half an hour ago, creating wildest fright and excitement. Elephant raged around streets; two plumbers going by, killed one — other escaped. Regret general.

O'FLAHERTY, *Detective*.

"Now he is right in the midst of my men," said the inspector. "Nothing can save him."

A succession of telegrams came from detectives who were scattered through New Jersey and Pennsylvania, and who were following clews consisting of ravaged barns, factories, and Sunday school libraries, with high hopes, — hopes amounting to certainties, indeed. The inspector said, —

"I wish I could communicate with them and order them north, but that is impossible. A detective only visits a telegraph office to send his report; then he is off again, and you don't know where to put your hand on him."

Now came this despatch: —

BRIDGEPORT, CT., 12.15.

Barnum offers rate of $4,000 a year for exclusive privilege of using elephant as travelling advertising medium from now till detectives find him. Wants to paste circus-posters on him. Desires immediate answer.

BOGGS, *Detective*.

"That is perfectly absurd!" I exclaimed.

"Of course it is," said the inspector. "Evidently Mr. Barnum, who thinks he is so sharp, does not know me, — but I know him."

Then he dictated this answer to the despatch: —

Mr. Barnum's offer declined. Make it $7,000 or nothing.

Chief BLUNT.

"There. We shall not have to wait long for an answer. Mr. Barnum is not at home; he is in the telegraph office, — it is his way when he has business on hand. Inside of three —"

DONE. — P. T. BARNUM.

So interrupted the clicking telegraphic instrument. Before I could make a comment upon this extraordinary episode, the following despatch carried my thoughts into another and very distressing channel:—

BOLIVIA, N. Y., 12.50.

Elephant arrived here from the south and passed through toward the forest at 11.50, dispersing a funeral on the way, and diminishing the mourners by two. Citizens fired some small cannon-balls into him, and then fled. Detective Burke and I arrived ten minutes later, from the north, but mistook some excavations for footprints, and so lost a good deal of time; but at last we struck the right trail and followed it to the woods. We then got down on our hands and knees and continued to keep a sharp eye on the track, and so shadowed it into the brush. Burke was in advance. Unfortunately the animal had stopped to rest; therefore, Burke having his head down, intent upon the track, butted up against the elephant's hind legs before he was aware of his vicinity. Burke instantly rose to his feet, seized the tail, and exclaimed joyfully, "I claim the re——" but got no further, for a single blow of the huge trunk laid the brave fellow's fragments low in death. I fled rearward, and the elephant turned and shadowed me to the edge of the wood, making tremendous speed, and I should inevitably have been lost, but that the remains of the funeral providentially intervened again and diverted his attention. I have just learned that nothing of that funeral is now left; but this is no loss, for there is an abundance of material for another. Meantime, the elephant has disappeared again.

MULROONEY, *Detective*.

We heard no news except from the diligent and confident detectives scattered about New Jersey, Pennsylvania, Delaware, and Virginia,—who were all following fresh and encouraging clews,—until shortly after 2 P.M., when this telegram came:—

BAXTER CENTRE, 2.15.

Elephant been here, plastered over with circus-bills, and broke up a revival, striking down and damaging many who were on the point of entering upon a better life. Citizens penned him up, and established a guard. When Detective Brown and I arrived, some time after, we entered enclosure and proceeded to identify elephant by photograph and description. All marks tallied exactly except one, which we could not see,—the boil-scar under armpit. To make sure, Brown crept under to look, and was immediately brained,—that is, head crushed and destroyed, though nothing issued from debris. All fled; so did elephant, striking right and left with much effect. Has escaped, but left bold blood-track from

cannon-wounds. Rediscovery certain. He broke southward, through a dense
forest.

BRENT, *Detective*.

That was the last telegram. At nightfall a fog shut down which was so
dense that objects but three feet away could not be discerned. This lasted
all night. The ferry-boats and even the omnibuses had to stop running.

III.

Next morning the papers were as full of detective theories as before;
they had all our tragic facts in detail also, and a great many more which
they had received from their telegraphic correspondents. Column after
column was occupied, a third of its way down, with glaring head-lines,
which it made my heart sick to read. Their general tone was like this: —

"THE WHITE ELEPHANT AT LARGE! HE MOVES UPON HIS FATAL MARCH!
WHOLE VILLAGES DESERTED BY THEIR FRIGHT-STRICKEN OCCUPANTS! PALE
TERROR GOES BEFORE HIM, DEATH AND DEVASTATION FOLLOW AFTER! AF-
TER THESE, THE DETECTIVES. BARNS DESTROYED, FACTORIES GUTTED, HAR-
VESTS DEVOURED, PUBLIC ASSEMBLAGES DISPERSED, ACCOMPANIED BY SCENES
OF CARNAGE IMPOSSIBLE TO DESCRIBE! THEORIES OF THIRTY-FOUR OF THE MOST
DISTINGUISHED DETECTIVES ON THE FORCE! THEORY OF CHIEF BLUNT!"

"There!" said Inspector Blunt, almost betrayed into excitement, "this
is magnificent! This is the greatest windfall that any detective organiza-
tion ever had. The fame of it will travel to the ends of the earth, and
endure to the end of time, and my name with it."

But there was no joy for me. I felt as if I had committed all those red
crimes, and that the elephant was only my irresponsible agent. And how
the list had grown! In one place he had "interfered with an election and
killed five repeaters." He had followed this act with the destruction of two
poor fellows, named O'Donohue and McFlannigan, who had "found a
refuge in the home of the oppressed of all lands only the day before, and
were in the act of exercising for the first time the noble right of American
citizens at the polls, when stricken down by the relentless hand of the
Scourge of Siam." In another, he had "found a crazy sensation-preacher
preparing his next season's heroic attacks on the dance, the theatre, and

other things which can't strike back, and had stepped on him." And in still another place he had "killed a lightning-rod agent." And so the list went on, growing redder and redder, and more and more heart-breaking. Sixty persons had been killed, and two hundred and forty wounded. All the accounts bore just testimony to the activity and devotion of the detectives, and all closed with the remark that "three hundred thousand citizens and four detectives saw the dread creature, and two of the latter he destroyed."

I dreaded to hear the telegraphic instrument begin to click again. By and by the messages began to pour in, but I was happily disappointed in their nature. It was soon apparent that all trace of the elephant was lost. The fog had enabled him to search out a good hiding-place unobserved. Telegrams from the most absurdly distant points reported that a dim vast mass had been glimpsed there through the fog at such and such an hour, and was "undoubtedly the elephant." This dim vast mass had been glimpsed in New Haven, in New Jersey, in Pennsylvania, in interior New York, in Brooklyn, and even in the city of New York itself! But in all cases the dim vast mass had vanished quickly and left no trace. Every detective of the large force scattered over this huge extent of country sent his hourly report, and each and every one of them had a clew, and was shadowing something, and was hot upon the heels of it.

But the day passed without other result.

The next day the same.

The next just the same.

The newspaper reports began to grow monotonous with facts that amounted to nothing, clews which led to nothing, and theories which had nearly exhausted the elements which surprise and delight and dazzle.

By advice of the inspector I doubled the reward.

Four more dull days followed. Then came a bitter blow to the poor, hard-working detectives,—the journalists declined to print their theories, and coldly said, "Give us a rest."

Two weeks after the elephant's disappearance I raised the reward to $75,000 by the inspector's advice. It was a great sum, but I felt that I would rather sacrifice my whole private fortune than lose my credit with my government. Now that the detectives were in adversity, the newspapers turned upon them, and began to fling the most stinging sarcasms at them. This gave the minstrels an idea, and they dressed themselves as detectives and hunted the elephant on the stage in the most extravagant way. The caricaturists made pictures of detectives scanning the country with spy-glasses, while the elephant, at their backs, stole apples out of their pockets. And they made all sorts of ridiculous pictures of the detective badge,—you have seen that badge printed in gold on the back of detective novels, no doubt,—it is a wide-staring eye, with the legend, "WE NEVER SLEEP." When detectives called for a drink, the would-be facetious bar-keeper resurrected an obsolete form of expression and said, "Will you have an eye-opener?" All the air was thick with sarcasms.

But there was one man who moved calm, untouched, unaffected, through it all. It was that heart of oak, the Chief Inspector. His brave eye never drooped, his serene confidence never wavered. He always said,—

"Let them rail on; he laughs best who laughs last."

My admiration for the man grew into a species of worship. I was at his side always. His office had become an unpleasant place to me, and now became daily more and more so. Yet if he could endure it I meant to do so also; at least, as long as I could. So I came regularly, and stayed,—the only outsider who seemed to be capable of it. Everybody wondered how I could; and often it seemed to me that I must desert, but at such times I looked into that calm and apparently unconscious face, and held my ground.

About three weeks after the elephant's disappearance I was about to say, one morning, that I should *have* to strike my colors and retire, when the great detective arrested the thought by proposing one more superb and masterly move.

This was to compromise with the robbers. The fertility of this man's invention exceeded anything I have ever seen, and I have had a wide intercourse with the world's finest minds. He said he was confident he could compromise for $100,000 and recover the elephant. I said I believed I could scrape the amount together, but what would become of the poor detectives who had worked so faithfully? He said,—

"In compromises they always get half."

This removed my only objection. So the inspector wrote two notes, in this form:—

DEAR MADAM,—Your husband can make a large sum of money (and be entirely protected from the law) by making an immediate appointment with me.
Chief BLUNT.

He sent one of these by his confidential messenger to the "reputed wife" of Brick Duffy, and the other to the reputed wife of Red McFadden.

Within the hour these offensive answers came:—

YE OWLD FOOL: brick McDuffys bin ded 2 yere.

BRIDGET MAHONEY.

CHIEF BAT,—Red McFadden is hung and in heving 18 month. Any Ass but a detective knose that.

MARY O'HOOLIGAN.

"I had long suspected these facts," said the inspector; "this testimony proves the unerring accuracy of my instinct."

The moment one resource failed him he was ready with another. He immediately wrote an advertisement for the morning papers, and I kept a copy of it:—

A.—xwblv. 242 N. Tjnd—fz328wmlg. Ozpo,—; 2 m! ogw. Mum.

He said that if the thief was alive this would bring him to the usual rendezvous. He further explained that the usual rendezvous was a place where all business affairs between detectives and criminals were conducted. This meeting would take place at twelve the next night.

We could do nothing till then, and I lost no time in getting out of the office, and was grateful indeed for the privilege.

At 11 the next night I brought $100,000 in bank-notes and put them into the chief's hands, and shortly afterward he took his leave, with the brave old undimmed confidence in his eye. An almost intolerable hour dragged to a close; then I heard his welcome tread, and rose gasping and tottered to meet him. How his fine eyes flamed with triumph! He said,—

"We've compromised! The jokers will sing a different tune to-morrow! Follow me!"

He took a lighted candle and strode down into the vast vaulted basement where sixty detectives always slept, and where a score were now playing cards to while the time. I followed close after him. He walked swiftly down to the dim remote end of the place, and just as I succumbed to the pangs of suffocation and was swooning away he stumbled and fell over the outlying members of a mighty object, and I heard him exclaim as he went down,—

"Our noble profession is vindicated. Here is your elephant!"

I was carried to the office above and restored with carbolic acid. The whole detective force swarmed in, and such another season of triumphant rejoicing ensued as I had never witnessed before. The reporters were called, baskets of champagne were opened, toasts were drunk, the handshakings and congratulations were continuous and enthusiastic. Naturally the chief was the hero of the hour, and his happiness was so complete and had been so patiently and worthily and bravely won that it made me happy to see it, though I stood there a homeless beggar, my priceless charge dead, and my position in my country's service lost to me through what would always seem my fatally careless execution of a great trust. Many an eloquent eye testified its deep admiration for the chief, and many a detective's voice murmured, "Look at him,—just the king of the profession,—only give him a clew, it's all he wants, and there ain't anything hid that he can't find." The dividing of the $50,000 made great pleasure; when it was finished the chief made a little speech while he put his share in his pocket, in which he said, "Enjoy it, boys, for you've earned it; and more than that you've earned for the detective profession undying fame."

A telegram arrived, which read:—

MONROE, MICH., 10 P. M.
First time I've struck a telegraph office in over three weeks. Have followed those footprints, horseback, through the woods, a thousand miles to here, and they get stronger and bigger and fresher every day. Don't worry—inside of another week I'll have the elephant. This is dead sure.

DARLEY, *Detective*.

The chief ordered three cheers for "Darley, one of the finest minds on the force," and then commanded that he be telegraphed to come home and receive his share of the reward.

So ended that marvellous episode of the stolen elephant. The newspapers were pleasant with praises once more, the next day, with one contemptible exception. This sheet said, "Great is the detective! He may be a little slow in finding a little thing like a mislaid elephant,—he may hunt him all day and sleep with his rotting carcass all night for three weeks, but he will find him at last—if he can get the man who mislaid him to show him the place!"

Poor Hassan was lost to me forever. The cannon-shots had wounded him fatally, he had crept to that unfriendly place in the fog, and there, surrounded by his enemies and in constant danger of detection, he had wasted away with hunger and suffering till death gave him peace.

The compromise cost me $100,000; my detective expenses were $42,000 more; I never applied for a place again under my government; I am a ruined man and a wanderer in the earth,—but my admiration for that man, whom I believe to be the greatest detective the world has ever produced, remains undimmed to this day, and will so remain unto the end.

The Private History of a Campaign that Failed

YOU HAVE HEARD from a great many people who did something in the war; is it not fair and right that you listen a little moment to one who started out to do something in it, but didn't? Thousands entered the war, got just a taste of it, and then stepped out again, permanently. These, by their very numbers, are respectable, and are therefore entitled to a sort of voice,—not a loud one, but a modest one; not a boastful one, but an apologetic one. They ought not to be allowed much space among better people—people who did something—I grant that; but they ought at least to be allowed to state why they didn't do anything, and also to explain the process by which they didn't do anything. Surely this kind of light must have a sort of value.

Out West there was a good deal of confusion in men's minds during the first months of the great trouble—a good deal of unsettledness, of leaning first this way, then that, then the other way. It was hard for us to get our bearings. I call to mind an instance of this. I was piloting on the

Mississippi when the news came that South Carolina had gone out of the Union on the 20th of December, 1860. My pilot-mate was a New Yorker. He was strong for the Union; so was I. But he would not listen to me with any patience; my loyalty was smirched, to his eye, because my father had owned slaves. I said, in palliation of this dark fact, that I had heard my father say, some years before he died, that slavery was a great wrong, and that he would free the solitary negro he then owned if he could think it right to give away the property of the family when he was so straitened in means. My mate retorted that a mere impulse was nothing—anybody could pretend to a good impulse; and went on decrying my Unionism and libeling my ancestry. A month later the secession atmosphere had considerably thickened on the Lower Mississippi, and I became a rebel; so did he. We were together in New Orleans, the 26th of January, when Louisiana went out of the Union. He did his full share of the rebel shouting, but was bitterly opposed to letting me do mine. He said that I came of bad stock—of a father who had been willing to set slaves free. In the following summer he was piloting a Federal gun-boat and shouting for the Union again, and I was in the Confederate army. I held his note for some borrowed money. He was one of the most upright men I ever knew; but he repudiated that note without hesitation, because I was a rebel, and the son of a man who owned slaves.

In that summer—of 1861—the first wash of the wave of war broke upon the shores of Missouri. Our State was invaded by the Union forces. They took possession of St. Louis, Jefferson Barracks, and some other points. The Governor, Claib Jackson, issued his proclamation calling out fifty thousand militia to repel the invader.

I was visiting in the small town where my boyhood had been spent—Hannibal, Marion County. Several of us got together in a se-cret place by night and formed ourselves into a military company. One Tom Lyman, a young fellow of a good deal of spirit but of no military experience, was made captain; I was made second lieutenant. We had no first lieutenant; I do not know why; it was long ago. There were fif-teen of us. By the advice of an innocent connected with the organiza-tion, we called ourselves the Marion Rangers. I do not remember that any one found fault with the name. I did not; I thought it sounded quite well. The young fellow who proposed this title was perhaps a fair sam-ple of the kind of stuff we were made of. He was young, ignorant, good-

The Seat of War.

natured, well-meaning, trivial, full of romance, and given to reading chivalric novels and singing forlorn love-ditties. He had some pathetic little nickel-plated aristocratic instincts, and detested his name, which was Dunlap; detested it, partly because it was nearly as common in that region as Smith, but mainly because it had a plebeian sound to his ear. So he tried to ennoble it by writing it in this way: *d' Unlap*. That contented his eye, but left his ear unsatisfied, for people gave the new name the same old pronunciation—emphasis on the front end of it. He then did the bravest thing that can be imagined,—a thing to make one shiver when one remembers how the world is given to resenting shams and affectations; he began to write his name so: *d' Un Lap*. And he waited patiently through the long storm of mud that was flung at this work of art, and he had his reward at last; for he lived to see that name accepted, and the emphasis put where he wanted it, by people who had known him all his life, and to whom the tribe of Dunlaps had been as familiar as the rain and the sunshine for forty years. So sure of victory at last is the courage that can wait. He said he had found, by consulting some ancient French chronicles, that the name was rightly and originally written d'Un Lap; and said that if it were translated into English it would mean Peterson: *Lap*, Latin or Greek, he said, for stone or rock, same as the French *pierre*, that is to say, Peter; *d'*, of or from; *un*, a or one; hence, d'Un Lap, of or from a stone or a Peter; that is to say, one who is the son of a stone, the son of a Peter—Peterson. Our militia company were not learned, and the explanation confused them; so they called him Peterson Dunlap. He proved useful to us in his way; he named our camps for us, and he generally struck a name that was "no slouch," as the boys said.

That is one sample of us. Another was Ed Stevens, son of the town jeweler,—trim-built, handsome, graceful, neat as a cat; bright, educated, but given over entirely to fun. There was nothing serious in life to him. As far as he was concerned, this military expedition of ours was simply a holiday. I should say that about half of us looked upon it in the same way; not consciously, perhaps, but unconsciously. We did not think; we were not capable of it. As for myself, I was full of unreasoning joy to be done with turning out of bed at midnight and four in the morning, for a while; grateful to have a change, new scenes, new occupations, a new interest. In my thoughts that was as far as I went; I did not go into the details; as a rule one doesn't at twenty-four.

Another sample was Smith, the blacksmith's apprentice. This vast donkey had some pluck, of a slow and sluggish nature, but a soft heart; at one time he would knock a horse down for some impropriety, and at another he would get homesick and cry. However, he had one ultimate credit to his account which some of us hadn't: he stuck to the war, and was killed in battle at last.

Jo Bowers, another sample, was a huge, good-natured, flax-headed lubber; lazy, sentimental, full of harmless brag, a grumbler by nature; an experienced, industrious, ambitious, and often quite picturesque liar, and yet not a successful one, for he had had no intelligent training, but was allowed to come up just any way. This life was serious enough to him, and seldom satisfactory. But he was a good fellow anyway, and the boys all liked him. He was made orderly sergeant; Stevens was made corporal.

These samples will answer—and they are quite fair ones. Well, this herd of cattle started for the war. What could you expect of them? They did as well as they knew how, but really what was justly to be expected of them? Nothing, I should say. That is what they did.

We waited for a dark night, for caution and secrecy were necessary; then, toward midnight, we stole in couples and from various directions to the Griffith place, beyond the town; from that point we set out together on foot. Hannibal lies at the extreme south-eastern corner of Marion County, on the Mississippi River; our objective point was the hamlet of New London, ten miles away, in Ralls County.

The first hour was all fun, all idle nonsense and laughter. But that could not be kept up. The steady trudging came to be like work; the play had somehow oozed out of it; the stillness of the woods and the somberness of the night began to throw a depressing influence over the spirits of the boys, and presently the talking died out and each person shut himself up in his own thoughts. During the last half of the second hour nobody said a word.

Now we approached a log farm-house where, according to report, there was a guard of five Union soldiers. Lyman called a halt; and there, in the deep gloom of the overhanging branches, he began to whisper a plan of assault upon that house, which made the gloom more depressing than it was before. It was a crucial moment; we realized, with a cold suddenness, that here was no jest—we were standing face to face with actual war. We were equal to the occasion. In our response there was no hesitation, no indecision: we said that if Lyman wanted to meddle with those soldiers, he could go ahead and do it; but if he waited for us to follow him, he would wait a long time.

Lyman urged, pleaded, tried to shame us, but it had no effect. Our course was plain, our minds were made up: we would flank the farm-house—go out around. And that is what we did.

We struck into the woods and entered upon a rough time, stumbling over roots, getting tangled in vines, and torn by briers. At last we reached an open place in a safe region, and sat down, blown and hot, to cool off and nurse our scratches and bruises. Lyman was annoyed, but the rest of us were cheerful; we had flanked the farm-house, we had made our first military movement, and it was a success; we had nothing to fret about, we were feeling just the other way. Horse-play and laughing began again; the expedition was become a holiday frolic once more.

Then we had two more hours of dull trudging and ultimate silence and depression; then, about dawn, we straggled into New London, soiled, heel-blistered, fagged with our little march, and all of us except Stevens in a sour and raspy humor and privately down on the war. We stacked our shabby old shot-guns in Colonel Ralls's barn, and then went in a body and breakfasted with that veteran of the Mexican war. Afterwards he took us to a distant meadow, and there in the shade of a tree we listened to an old-fashioned speech from him, full of gunpowder and glory, full of that adjective-piling, mixed metaphor, and windy declamation which was regarded as eloquence in that ancient time and that remote region; and then he swore us on the Bible to be faithful to the State of Missouri and drive all invaders from her soil, no matter whence they might come or under what flag they might march. This mixed us considerably, and we could not make out just what service we were embarked in; but Colonel Ralls, the practiced politician and phrase-juggler, was not similarly in doubt; he knew quite clearly that he had invested us in the cause of the Southern Confederacy. He closed the solemnities by belting around me the sword which his neighbor, Colonel Brown, had worn at Buena Vista and Molino del Rey; and he accompanied this act with another impressive blast.

Then we formed in line of battle and marched four miles to a shady and pleasant piece of woods on the border of the far-reaching expanses of a flowery prairie. It was an enchanting region for war — our kind of war.

We pierced the forest about half a mile, and took up a strong position, with some low, rocky, and wooded hills behind us, and a purling, limpid creek in front. Straightway half the command were in swimming, and the other half fishing. The ass with the French name gave this position a romantic title, but it was too long, so the boys shortened and simplified it to Camp Ralls.

We occupied an old maple-sugar camp, whose half-rotted troughs were still propped against the trees. A long corn-crib served for sleeping quarters for the battalion. On our left, half a mile away, was Mason's farm and house; and he was a friend to the cause. Shortly after noon the farmers began to arrive from several directions, with mules and horses for our use, and these they lent us for as long as the war might last, which they judged would be about three months. The animals were of all sizes, all colors, and all breeds. They were mainly young and frisky, and nobody in the command could stay on them long at a time; for we were town boys, and ignorant of horsemanship. The creature that fell to my share was a very small mule, and yet so quick and active that it could throw me without difficulty; and it did this whenever I got on it. Then it would bray—stretching its neck out, laying its ears back, and spreading its jaws till you could see down to its works. It was a disagreeable animal, in every way. If I took it by the bridle and tried to lead it off the grounds, it would sit down and brace back, and no one could budge it. However, I was not entirely destitute of military resources, and I did presently manage to spoil this game; for I had seen many a steamboat aground in my time, and knew a trick or two which even a grounded mule would be obliged to respect. There was a well by the corn-crib; so I substituted thirty fathom of rope for the bridle, and fetched him home with the windlass.

I will anticipate here sufficiently to say that we did learn to ride, after some days' practice, but never well. We could not learn to like our animals; they were not choice ones, and most of them had annoying peculiarities of one kind or another. Stevens's horse would carry him, when he was not noticing, under the huge excrescences which form on the trunks of oak-trees, and wipe him out of the saddle; in this way Stevens got several bad hurts. Sergeant Bowers's horse was very large and tall, with slim, long legs, and looked like a railroad bridge. His size enabled him to reach all about, and as far as he wanted to, with his head; so he was always biting Bowers's legs. On the march, in the sun, Bowers slept a good deal; and as soon as the horse recognized that he was asleep he would reach around and bite him on the leg. His legs were black and blue with bites. This was the only thing that could ever make him swear, but this always did; whenever the horse bit him he always swore, and of course Stevens, who laughed at everything, laughed at this, and would even get into such convulsions over it as to lose his balance and fall off his horse; and then Bowers, already irritated by the pain of the horse-bite, would resent the laughter with hard language, and there would be a quarrel; so that horse made no end of trouble and bad blood in the command.

However, I will get back to where I was—our first afternoon in the sugar-camp. The sugar-troughs came very handy as horse-troughs, and we had plenty of corn to fill them with. I ordered Sergeant Bowers to feed my mule; but he said that if I reckoned he went to war to be dry-nurse to a mule, it wouldn't take me very long to find out my mistake. I believed that this was insubordination, but I was full of uncertainties about everything military, and so I let the thing pass, and went and ordered Smith, the blacksmith's apprentice, to feed the mule; but he merely gave me a large, cold, sarcastic grin, such as an ostensibly seven-year-old horse gives you when you lift his lip and find he is fourteen, and turned his back on me. I then went to the captain, and asked if it was not right and proper and military for me to have an orderly. He said it was, but as there was only one orderly in the corps, it was but right that he himself should have Bowers on his staff. Bowers said he wouldn't serve on anybody's staff; and if anybody thought he could make him, let him try it. So, of course, the thing had to be dropped; there was no other way.

Next, nobody would cook; it was considered a degradation; so we had no dinner. We lazied the rest of the pleasant afternoon away, some dozing under the trees, some smoking cob-pipes and talking sweet-hearts and war, some playing games. By late supper-time all hands were famished; and to meet the difficulty all hands turned to, on an equal footing, and gathered wood, built fires, and cooked the meal. Afterward everything was smooth for a while; then trouble broke out between the corporal and the sergeant, each claiming to rank the other. Nobody knew which was the higher office; so Lyman had to settle the matter by making the rank of both officers equal. The commander of an ignorant crew like that has many troubles and vexations which probably do not occur in the regular army at all. However, with the song-singing and yarn-spinning around the camp-fire, everything presently became serene again; and by and by we raked the corn down level in one end of the crib, and all went to bed on it, tying a horse to the door, so that he would neigh if any one tried to get in.*

---

* It was always my impression that that was what the horse was there for, and I know that it was also the impression of at least one other of the command, for we talked about it at the time, and admired the military ingenuity of the device; but when I was out West three years ago I was told by Mr. A. G. Fuqua, a member of our company, that the horse was his, that the leaving him tied at the door was a matter of mere forgetfulness, and that to attribute it to intelligent invention was to give him quite too much credit. In support of his position, he called my attention to the suggestive fact that the artifice was not employed again. I had not thought of that before.

We had some horsemanship drill every forenoon; then, afternoons, we rode off here and there in squads a few miles, and visited the farmers' girls, and had a youthful good time, and got an honest good dinner or supper, and then home again to camp, happy and content.

For a time, life was idly delicious, it was perfect; there was nothing to mar it. Then came some farmers with an alarm one day. They said it was rumored that the enemy were advancing in our direction, from over Hyde's prairie. The result was a sharp stir among us, and general consternation. It was a rude awakening from our pleasant trance. The rumor was but a rumor—nothing definite about it; so, in the confusion, we did not know which way to retreat. Lyman was for not retreating at all, in these uncertain circumstances; but he found that if he tried to maintain that attitude he would fare badly, for the command were in no humor to put up with insubordination. So he yielded the point and called a council of war—to consist of himself and the three other officers; but the privates made such a fuss about being left out, that we had to allow them to be present. I mean we had to allow them to remain, for they were already present, and doing the most of the talking too. The question was, which way to retreat; but all were so flurried that nobody seemed to have even a guess to offer. Except Lyman. He explained in a few calm words, that inasmuch as the enemy were approaching from over Hyde's prairie, our course was simple: all we had to do was not to retreat *toward* him; any other direction would answer our needs perfectly. Everybody saw in a moment how true this was, and how wise; so Lyman got a great many compliments. It was now decided that we should fall back on Mason's farm.

It was after dark by this time, and as we could not know how soon the enemy might arrive, it did not seem best to try to take the horses and things with us; so we only took the guns and ammunition, and started at once. The route was very rough and hilly and rocky, and presently the night grew very black and rain began to fall; so we had a troublesome time of it, struggling and stumbling along in the dark; and soon some person slipped and fell, and then the next person behind stumbled over him and fell, and so did the rest, one after the other; and then Bowers came with the keg of powder in his arms, whilst the command were all mixed together, arms and legs, on the muddy slope; and so he fell, of course, with the keg, and this started the whole detachment down the

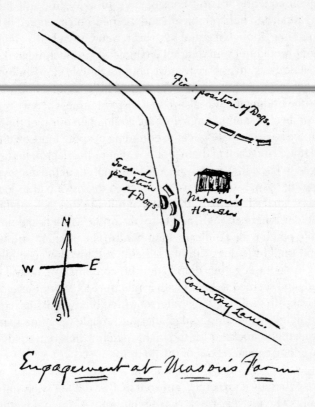

Engagement at Mason's Farm

hill in a body, and they landed in the brook at the bottom in a pile, and each that was undermost pulling the hair and scratching and biting those that were on top of him; and those that were being scratched and bitten scratching and biting the rest in their turn, and all saying they would die before they would ever go to war again if they ever got out of this brook this time, and the invader might rot for all they cared, and the country along with him — and all such talk as that, which was dismal to hear and take part in, in such smothered, low voices, and such a grisly dark place and so wet, and the enemy may be coming any moment.

The keg of powder was lost, and the guns too; so the growling and complaining continued straight along whilst the brigade pawed around the pasty hillside and slopped around in the brook hunting for these things; consequently we lost considerable time at this; and then we heard a sound, and held our breath and listened, and it seemed to be the enemy coming, though it could have been a cow, for it had a cough like a cow; but we did not wait, but left a couple of guns behind and struck out for Mason's again as briskly as we could scramble along in the dark. But we got lost presently among the rugged little ravines, and wasted a deal of time finding the way again, so it was after nine when we reached Mason's stile at last; and then before we could open our mouths to give the countersign, several dogs came bounding over the fence, with great riot and noise, and each of them took a soldier by the slack of his trousers and began to back away with him. We could not shoot the dogs without endangering the persons they were attached to; so we had to look on, helpless, at what was perhaps the most mortifying spectacle of the civil war. There was light enough, and to spare, for the Masons had now run out on the porch with candles in their hands. The old man and his son came and undid the dogs without difficulty, all but Bowers's; but they couldn't undo his dog, they didn't know his combination; he was of the bull kind, and seemed to be set with a Yale time-lock; but they got him loose at last with some scalding water, of which Bowers got his share and returned thanks. Peterson Dunlap afterwards made up a fine name for this engagement, and also for the night march which preceded it, but both have long ago faded out of my memory.

We now went into the house, and they began to ask us a world of questions, whereby it presently came out that we did not know anything concerning who or what we were running from; so the old gentleman made himself very frank, and said we were a curious breed of soldiers, and guessed we could be depended on to end up the war in time, because no government could stand the expense of the shoe-leather we should cost it trying to follow us around. "Marion *Rangers!* good name, b'gosh!" said he. And wanted to know why we hadn't had a picket-guard at the place where the road entered the prairie, and why we hadn't sent out a scouting party to spy out the enemy and bring us an account of his strength, and so on, before jumping up and stampeding out of a strong position upon a mere vague rumor—and so on and so forth, till he made us all feel shabbier than the dogs had done, not half so enthusiastically welcome. So we went to bed shamed and low-spirited; except Stevens. Soon Stevens began to devise a garment for Bowers which could be made to automatically display his battle-scars to the grateful, or conceal them from the envious, according to his occasions; but Bowers was in no humor for this, so there was a fight, and when it was over Stevens had some battle-scars of his own to think about.

Then we got a little sleep. But after all we had gone through, our activities were not over for the night; for about two o'clock in the morning we heard a shout of warning from down the lane, accompanied by a chorus from all the dogs, and in a moment everybody was up and flying around to find out what the alarm was about. The alarmist was a horseman who gave notice that a detachment of Union soldiers was on its way from Hannibal with orders to capture and hang any bands like ours which it could find, and said we had no time to lose. Farmer Mason was in a flurry this time, himself. He hurried us out of the house with all haste, and sent one of his negroes with us to show us where to hide ourselves and our tell-tale guns among the ravines half a mile away. It was raining heavily.

We struck down the lane, then across some rocky pasture-land which offered good advantages for stumbling; consequently we were down in the mud most of the time, and every time a man went down he blackguarded the war, and the people that started it, and everybody connected with it, and gave himself the master dose of all for being so foolish as to go into it. At last we reached the wooded mouth of a ravine, and there we huddled ourselves under the streaming trees, and sent the negro back home. It was a dismal and heart-breaking time. We were like to be drowned with the rain, deafened with the howling wind and the booming thunder, and blinded by the lightning. It was indeed a wild night. The drenching we were getting was misery enough, but a deeper misery still was the reflection that the halter might end us before we were a day older. A death of this shameful sort had not occurred to us as being among the possibilities of war. It took the romance all out of the campaign, and turned our dreams of glory into a repulsive nightmare. As for doubting that so barbarous an order had been given, not one of us did that.

The long night wore itself out at last, and then the negro came to us with the news that the alarm had manifestly been a false one, and that breakfast would soon be ready. Straightway we were lighted-hearted again, and the world was bright, and life as full of hope and promise as ever—for we were young then. How long ago that was! Twenty-four years.

The mongrel child of philology named the night's refuge Camp Devastation, and no soul objected. The Masons gave us a Missouri country breakfast, in Missourian abundance, and we needed it: hot biscuits; hot "wheat bread" prettily criss-crossed in a lattice pattern on top; hot corn pone; fried chicken; bacon, coffee, eggs, milk, buttermilk, etc.;—and the world may be confidently challenged to furnish the equal to such a breakfast, as it is cooked in the South.

We staid several days at Mason's; and after all these years the memory of the dullness, the stillness and lifelessness of that slumberous farmhouse still oppresses my spirit as with a sense of the presence of death and mourning. There was nothing to do, nothing to think about; there was no interest in life. The male part of the household were away in the fields all day, the women were busy and out of our sight; there was no sound but the plaintive wailing of a spinning-wheel, forever moaning out from some distant room,—the most lonesome sound in nature, a sound steeped and sodden with homesickness and the emptiness of life. The family went to bed about dark every night, and as we were not invited to intrude any new customs, we naturally followed theirs. Those nights were a hundred years long to youths accustomed to being up till twelve. We lay awake and miserable till that hour every time, and grew old and decrepit waiting through the still eternities for the clock-strikes. This was no place for town boys. So at last it was with something very like joy that we received news that the enemy were on our track again. With a new birth of the old warrior spirit, we sprang to our places in line of battle and fell back on Camp Ralls.

Captain Lyman had taken a hint from Mason's talk, and he now gave orders that our camp should be guarded against surprise by the posting of pickets. I was ordered to place a picket at the forks of the road in Hyde's prairie. Night shut down black and threatening. I told Sergeant Bowers to go out to that place and stay till midnight; and, just as I was expecting, he said he wouldn't do it. I tried to get others to go, but all refused. Some excused themselves on account of the weather; but the rest were frank enough to say they wouldn't go in any kind of weather. This kind of thing sounds odd now, and impossible, but there was no surprise in it at the time. On the contrary, it seemed a perfectly natural thing to do. There were scores of little camps scattered over Missouri where the same thing was happening. These camps were composed of young men who had been born and reared to a sturdy independence, and who did not know what it meant to be ordered around by Tom, Dick, and Harry, whom they had known familiarly all their lives, in the village or on the farm. It is quite within the probabilities that this same thing was happening all over the South. James Redpath recognized the justice of this assumption, and furnished the following instance in support of it. During a short stay in East Tennessee he was in a citizen colonel's tent one day, talking, when a big private appeared at the door, and without salute or other circumlocution said to the colonel:

"Say, Jim, I'm a-goin' home for a few days."

"What for?"

"Well, I hain't b'en there for a right smart while, and I'd like to see how things is comin' on."

"How long are you going to be gone?"

" 'Bout two weeks."

"Well, don't be gone longer than that; and get back sooner if you can."

That was all, and the citizen officer resumed his conversation where the private had broken it off. This was in the first months of the war, of course. The camps in our part of Missouri were under Brigadier-General Thomas H. Harris. He was a townsman of ours, a first-rate fellow, and well liked; but we had all familiarly known him as the sole and modest-salaried operator in our telegraph office, where he had to send about one dispatch a week in ordinary times, and two when there was a rush of business; consequently, when he appeared in our midst one day, on the wing, and delivered a military command of some sort, in a large military fashion, nobody was surprised at the response which he got from the assembled soldiery:

"Oh, now, what'll you take to *don't*, Tom Harris!"

It was quite the natural thing. One might justly imagine that we were hopeless material for war. And so we seemed, in our ignorant state; but there were those among us who afterward learned the grim trade; learned to obey like machines; became valuable soldiers; fought all through the war, and came out at the end with excellent records. One of the very boys who refused to go out on picket duty that night, and called me an ass for thinking he would expose himself to danger in such a foolhardy way, had become distinguished for intrepidity before he was a year older.

I did secure my picket that night—not by authority, but by diplomacy. I got Bowers to go, by agreeing to exchange ranks with him for the time being, and go along and stand the watch with him as his subordinate. We staid out there a couple of dreary hours in the pitchy darkness and the rain, with nothing to modify the dreariness but Bowers's monotonous growlings at the war and the weather; then we began to nod, and presently found it next to impossible to stay in the saddle; so we gave up the tedious job, and went back to the camp without waiting for the relief guard. We rode into camp without interruption or objection from anybody, and the enemy could have done the same, for there were no sentries. Everybody was asleep; at midnight there was nobody to send out another picket, so none was sent. We never tried to establish a watch at night again, as far as I remember, but we generally kept a picket out in the daytime.

In that camp the whole command slept on the corn in the big corn-crib; and there was usually a general row before morning, for the place was full of rats, and they would scramble over the boys' bodies and faces, annoying and irritating everybody; and now and then they would bite some one's toe, and the person who owned the toe would start up and magnify his English and begin to throw corn in the dark. The ears were half as heavy as bricks, and when they struck they hurt. The persons struck would respond, and inside of five minutes every man would be locked in a death-grip with his neighbor. There was a grievous deal of blood shed in the corn-crib, but this was all that was spilt while I was in the war. No, that is not quite true. But for one circumstance it would have been all. I will come to that now.

Our scares were frequent. Every few days rumors would come that the enemy were approaching. In these cases we always fell back on some other camp of ours; we never staid where we were. But the rumors always turned out to be false; so at last even we began to grow indifferent to them. One night a negro was sent to our corn-crib with the same old warning: the enemy was hovering in our neighborhood. We all said let him hover. We resolved to stay still and be comfortable. It was a fine warlike resolution, and no doubt we all felt the stir of it in our veins—for a moment. We had been having a very jolly time, that was full of horse-play and school-boy hilarity; but that cooled down now, and presently the fast-waning-fire of forced jokes and forced laughs died out altogether, and the company became silent. Silent and nervous. And soon uneasy—worried—apprehensive. We had said we would stay, and we were committed. We could have been persuaded to go, but there was nobody brave enough to suggest it. An almost noiseless movement presently began in the dark, by a general but unvoiced impulse. When the movement was completed, each man knew that he was not the only person who had crept to the front wall and had his eye at a crack between the logs. No, we were all there; all there with our hearts in our throats, and staring out toward the sugar-troughs where the forest foot-path came through. It was late, and there was a deep woodsy stillness everywhere. There was a veiled moonlight, which was only just strong enough to enable us to mark the general shape of objects. Presently a muffled sound caught our ears, and we recognized it as the hoof-beats of a horse or horses. And right away a figure appeared in the forest path; it could have been made of smoke, its mass had so little sharpness of outline. It was a man on horseback; and it seemed to me that there were others behind him. I got hold of a gun in the dark, and pushed it through a crack between the logs, hardly knowing what I was doing, I was so dazed with fright. Somebody said "Fire!" I pulled the trigger. I seemed to see a hundred flashes and hear a hundred reports, then I saw the man fall down out of the saddle. My first feeling was of surprised gratification; my first impulse was an apprentice-sportsman's impulse to run and pick up his game. Somebody said, hardly audibly, "Good—we've got him!—wait for the rest." But the rest did not come. We waited—listened—still no more came. There was not a sound, not the whisper of a leaf; just perfect stillness; an uncanny kind of stillness, which was all the more uncanny on account of the damp, earthy, late-night smells now rising and pervading it. Then, wondering, we crept stealthily out, and approached the man. When we got to him the moon revealed him distinctly. He was lying on his back, with his arms abroad; his mouth was open and his chest heaving with long gasps, and his white shirt-front was all splashed with blood. The thought shot through me that I was a murderer; that I had killed a man—a man who had never done me any harm. That was the coldest sensation that ever went through my marrow. I was down by him in a moment, helplessly stroking his forehead; and I would have given anything then—my own life freely—to make him again what he had been five minutes before. And all the boys seemed to be feeling in the same way; they hung over him, full of pitying interest, and tried all they could to help him, and said all sorts of regretful things. They had forgotten all about the enemy; they thought only of this one forlorn unit of the foe. Once my imagination persuaded me that the dying man gave me a reproachful look out of his shadowy eyes, and it seemed to me that I could rather he had stabbed me than done that. He muttered and mumbled like a dreamer in his sleep, about his wife and his child; and I thought with a new despair, "This thing that I have done does not end with him; it falls upon *them* too, and they never did me any harm, any more than he."

In a little while the man was dead. He was killed in war; killed in fair and legitimate war; killed in battle, as you may say; and yet he was as sincerely mourned by the opposing force as if he had been their brother. The boys stood there a half hour sorrowing over him, and recalling the details of the tragedy, and wondering who he might be, and if he were a spy, and saying that if it were to do over again they would not hurt him unless he attacked them first. It soon came out that mine was not the only shot fired; there were five others,—a division of the guilt which was a grateful relief to me, since it in some degree lightened and diminished the burden I was carrying. There were six shots fired at once; but I was not in my right mind at the time, and my heated imagination had magnified my one shot into a volley.

The man was not in uniform, and was not armed. He was a stranger in the country; that was all we ever found out about him. The thought of him got to preying upon me every night; I could not get rid of it. I could not drive it away, the taking of that unoffending life seemed such a wanton thing. And it seemed an epitome of war; that all war must be just that—the killing of strangers against whom you feel no personal animosity; strangers whom, in other circumstances, you would help if you found them in trouble, and who would help you if you needed it. My campaign was spoiled. It seemed to me that I was not rightly equipped for this awful business; that war was intended for men, and I for a child's nurse. I resolved to retire from this avocation of sham soldiership while I could save some remnant of my self-respect. These morbid thoughts clung to me against reason; for at bottom I did not believe I had touched that man. The law of probabilities decreed me guiltless of his blood; for in all my small experience with guns I had never hit anything I had tried to hit, and I knew I had done my best to hit him. Yet there was no solace in the thought. Against a diseased imagination, demonstration goes for nothing.

The rest of my war experience was of a piece with what I have already told of it. We kept monotonously falling back upon one camp or another, and eating up the country. I marvel now at the patience of the farmers and their families. They ought to have shot us; on the contrary, they were as hospitably kind and courteous to us as if we had deserved it. In one of these camps we found Ab Grimes, an Upper Mississippi pilot, who afterwards became famous as a dare-devil rebel spy, whose career bristled with desperate adventures. The look and style of his comrades suggested that they had not come into the war to play, and their deeds made good the conjecture later. They were fine horsemen and good revolver-shots; but their favorite arm was the lasso. Each had one at his pommel, and could snatch a man out of the saddle with it every time, on a full gallop, at any reasonable distance.

In another camp the chief was a fierce and profane old blacksmith of sixty, and he had furnished his twenty recruits with gigantic home-made bowie-knives, to be swung with the two hands, like the *machetes* of the Isthmus. It was a grisly spectacle to see that earnest band practicing their murderous cuts and slashes under the eye of that remorseless old fanatic.

The last camp which we fell back upon was in a hollow near the village of Florida, where I was born—in Monroe County. Here we were warned, one day, that a Union colonel was sweeping down on us with a whole regiment at his heels. This looked decidedly serious. Our boys went apart and consulted; then we went back and told the other companies present that the war was a disappointment to us and we were going to disband. They were getting ready, themselves, to fall back on some place or other, and were only waiting for General Tom Harris, who was expected to arrive at any moment; so they tried to persuade us to wait a little while, but the majority of us said no, we were accustomed to falling back, and didn't need any of Tom Harris's help; we could get along perfectly well without him—and save time too. So about half of our fifteen, including myself, mounted and left on the instant; the others yielded to persuasion and staid—staid through the war.

An hour later we met General Harris on the road, with two or three people in his company—his staff, probably, but we could not tell; none of them were in uniform; uniforms had not come into vogue among us yet. Harris ordered us back; but we told him there was a Union colonel coming with a whole regiment in his wake, and it looked as if there was going to be a disturbance; so we had concluded to go home. He raged a little, but it was of no use; our minds were made up. We had done our share; had killed one man, exterminated one army, such as it was; let him go and kill the rest, and that would end the war. I did not see that brisk young general again until last year; then he was wearing white hair and whiskers.

In time I came to know that Union colonel whose coming frightened me out of the war and crippled the Southern cause to that extent—General Grant. I came within a few hours of seeing him when he was as unknown as I was myself; at a time when anybody could have said, "Grant?—Ulysses S. Grant? I do not remember hearing the name before." It seems difficult to realize that there was once a time when such a remark could be rationally made; but there *was*, and I was within a few miles of the place and the occasion too, though proceeding in the other direction.

The thoughtful will not throw this war-paper of mine lightly aside as being valueless. It has this value: it is a not unfair picture of what went on in many and many a militia camp in the first months of the rebellion, when the green recruits were without discipline, without the steadying and heartening influence of trained leaders; when all their circumstances were new and strange, and charged with exaggerated terrors, and before the invaluable experience of actual collision in the field had turned them from rabbits into soldiers. If this side of the picture of that early day has not before been put into history, then history has been to that degree incomplete, for it had and has its rightful place there. There was more Bull Run material scattered through the early camps of this country than exhibited itself at Bull Run. And yet it learned its trade presently, and helped to fight the great battles later. I could have become a soldier myself, if I had waited. I had got part of it learned; I knew more about retreating than the man that invented retreating.

Fenimore Cooper's Literary Offences

The Pathfinder and *The Deerslayer* stand at the head of Cooper's novels as artistic creations. There are others of his works which contain parts as perfect as are to be found in these, and scenes even more thrilling. Not one can be compared with either of them as a finished whole.

The defects in both of these tales are comparatively slight. They were pure works of art.—*Prof. Lounsbury*.

The five tales reveal an extraordinary fulness of invention.

. . . One of the very greatest characters in fiction, "Natty Bumppo." . . .

The craft of the woodsman, the tricks of the trapper, all the delicate art of the forest, were familiar to Cooper from his youth up.—*Prof. Brander Matthews*.

Cooper is the greatest artist in the domain of romantic fiction yet produced by America.—*Wilkie Collins*.

IT SEEMS to me that it was far from right for the Professor of English Literature in Yale, the Professor of English Literature in Columbia, and Wilkie Collins, to deliver opinions on Cooper's literature without having read some of it. It would have been much more decorous to keep silent and let persons talk who have read Cooper.

Cooper's art has some defects. In one place in *Deerslayer*, and in the restricted space of two-thirds of a page, Cooper has scored 114 offences against literary art out of a possible 115. It breaks the record.

There are nineteen rules governing literary art in the domain of romantic fiction—some say twenty-two. In *Deerslayer* Cooper violated eighteen of them. These eighteen require:

1.   That a tale shall accomplish something and arrive somewhere. But the *Deerslayer* tale accomplishes nothing and arrives in the air.

2.   They require that the episodes of a tale shall be necessary parts of the tale, and shall help to develop it. But as the *Deerslayer* tale is not a tale, and accomplishes nothing and arrives nowhere, the episodes have no rightful place in the work, since there was nothing for them to develop.

3.   They require that the personages in a tale shall be alive, except in the case of corpses, and that always the reader shall be able to tell the corpses from the others. But this detail has often been overlooked in the *Deerslayer* tale.

4.   They require that the personages in a tale, both dead and alive,

shall exhibit a sufficient excuse for being there. But this detail also has been overlooked in the *Deerslayer* tale.

5. They require that when the personages of a tale deal in conversation, the talk shall sound like human talk, and be talk such as human beings would be likely to talk in the given circumstances, and have a discoverable meaning, also a discoverable purpose, and a show of relevancy, and remain in the neighborhood of the subject in hand, and be interesting to the reader, and help out the tale, and stop when the people cannot think of anything more to say. But this requirement has been ignored from the beginning of the *Deerslayer* tale to the end of it.

6. They require that when the author describes the character of a personage in his tale, the conduct and conversation of that personage shall justify said description. But this law gets little or no attention in the *Deerslayer* tale, as "Natty Bumppo's" case will amply prove.

7. They require that when a personage talks like an illustrated, gilt-edged, tree-calf, hand-tooled, seven-dollar Friendship's Offering in the beginning of a paragraph, he shall not talk like a negro minstrel in the end of it. But this rule is flung down and danced upon in the *Deerslayer* tale.

8. They require that crass stupidities shall not be played upon the reader as "the craft of the woodsman, the delicate art of the forest," by either the author or the people in the tale. But this rule is persistently violated in the *Deerslayer* tale.

9. They require that the personages of a tale shall confine themselves to possibilities and let miracles alone; or, if they venture a miracle, the author must so plausibly set it forth as to make it look possible and reasonable. But these rules are not respected in the *Deerslayer* tale.

10. They require that the author shall make the reader feel a deep interest in the personages of his tale and in their fate; and that he shall make the reader love the good people in the tale and hate the bad ones. But the reader of the *Deerslayer* tale dislikes the good people in it, is indifferent to the others, and wishes they would all get drowned together.

11. They require that the characters in a tale shall be so clearly defined that the reader can tell beforehand what each will do in a given emergency. But in the *Deerslayer* tale this rule is vacated.

In addition to these large rules there are some little ones. These require that the author shall

12.   *Say* what he is proposing to say, not merely come near it.
13.   Use the right word, not its second cousin.
14.   Eschew surplusage.
15.   Not omit necessary details.
16.   Avoid slovenliness of form.
17.   Use good grammar.
18.   Employ a simple and straightforward style.

Even these seven are coldly and persistently violated in the *Deerslayer* tale.

Cooper's gift in the way of invention was not a rich endowment; but such as it was he liked to work it, he was pleased with the effects, and indeed he did some quite sweet things with it. In his little box of stage properties he kept six or eight cunning devices, tricks, artifices for his savages and woodsmen to deceive and circumvent each other with, and he was never so happy as when he was working these innocent things and seeing them go. A favorite one was to make a moccasined person tread in the tracks of the moccasined enemy, and thus hide his own trail. Cooper wore out barrels and barrels of moccasins in working that trick. Another stage-property that he pulled out of his box pretty frequently was his broken twig. He prized his broken twig above all the rest of his effects, and worked it the hardest. It is a restful chapter in any book of his when somebody doesn't step on a dry twig and alarm all the reds and whites for two hundred yards around. Every time a Cooper person is in peril, and absolute silence is worth four dollars a minute, he is sure to step on a dry twig. There may be a hundred handier things to step on, but that wouldn't satisfy Cooper. Cooper requires him to turn out and find a dry twig; and if he can't do it, go and borrow one. In fact the Leather Stocking Series ought to have been called the Broken Twig Series.

I am sorry there is not room to put in a few dozen instances of the delicate art of the forest, as practiced by Natty Bumppo and some of the other Cooperian experts. Perhaps we may venture two or three samples. Cooper was a sailor—a naval officer; yet he gravely tells us how a vessel, driving toward a lee shore in a gale, is steered for a particular spot by her skipper because he knows of an *undertow* there which will hold her back against the gale and save her. For just pure woodcraft, or sailorcraft, or whatever it is, isn't that neat? For several years Cooper was daily in the society of artillery, and he ought to have noticed that when a cannon ball strikes the ground it either buries itself or skips a hundred feet or so; skips again a hundred feet or so—and so on, till it finally gets tired and rolls. Now in one place he loses some "females"—as he always calls women—in the edge of a wood near a plain at night in a fog, on purpose to give Bumppo a chance to show off the delicate art of the forest before the reader. These mislaid people are hunting for a fort. They hear a cannon-blast, and a cannon-ball presently comes rolling into the wood and stops at their feet. To the females this suggests nothing. The case is very different with the admirable Bumppo. I wish I may never know peace again if he doesn't strike out promptly and *follow the track* of that cannon-ball across the plain through the dense fog and find the fort. Isn't it a daisy? If Cooper had any real knowledge of Nature's ways of doing things, he had a most delicate art in concealing the fact. For instance: one of his acute Indian experts, Chingachgook (pronounced Chicago, I think), has lost the trail of a person he is tracking through the forest. Apparently that trail is hopelessly lost. Neither you nor I could ever have guessed out the way to find it. It was very different with Chicago. Chicago was not stumped for long. He turned a running stream out of its course, and there, in the slush in its old bed, were that person's moccasin-tracks. The current did not wash them away, as it would have done in all other like cases—no, even the eternal laws of Nature have to vacate when Cooper wants to put up a delicate job of woodcraft on the reader.

We must be a little wary when Brander Matthews tells us that Cooper's books "reveal an extraordinary fulness of invention." As a rule, I am quite willing to accept Brander Matthews's literary judgments and applaud his lucid and graceful phrasing of them; but that particular statement needs to be taken with a few tons of salt. Bless your heart, Cooper hadn't any more invention than a horse; and I don't mean a high-class horse, either; I mean a clothes-horse. It would be very difficult to find a really clever "situation" in Cooper's books; and still more difficult to find one of any kind which he has failed to render absurd by his handling of it. Look at the episodes of "the caves;" and at the celebrated scuffle between Magua and those others on the table-land a few days later; and at Hurry Harry's queer water-transit from the castle to the ark; and at Deerslayer's half hour with his first corpse; and at the quarrel between

Hurry Harry and Deerslayer later; and at—but choose for yourself; you can't go amiss.

If Cooper had been an observer, his inventive faculty would have worked better, not more interestingly, but more rationally, more plausibly. Cooper's proudest creations in the way of "situations" suffer noticeably from the absence of the observer's protecting gift. Cooper's eye was splendidly inaccurate. Cooper seldom saw anything correctly. He saw nearly all things as through a glass eye, darkly. Of course a man who cannot see the commonest little everyday matters accurately is working at a disadvantage when he is constructing a "situation." In the *Deerslayer* tale Cooper has a stream which is fifty feet wide, where it flows out of a lake; it presently narrows to twenty as it meanders along for no given reason, and yet, when a stream acts like that it ought to be required to explain itself. Fourteen pages later the width of the brook's outlet from the lake has suddenly shrunk thirty feet, and become "the narrowest part of the stream." This shrinkage is not accounted for. The stream has bends in it, a sure indication that it has alluvial banks, and cuts them; yet these bends are only thirty and fifty feet long. If Cooper had been a nice and punctilious observer he would have noticed that the bends were oftener nine hundred feet long than short of it.

Cooper made the exit of that stream fifty feet wide in the first place, for no particular reason; in the second place, he narrowed it to less than twenty to accommodate some Indians. He bends a "sapling" to the form of an arch over this narrow passage, and conceals six Indians in its foliage. They are "laying" for a settler's scow or ark which is coming up the stream on its way to the lake; it is being hauled against the stiff current by a rope whose stationary end is anchored in the lake; its rate of progress cannot be more than a mile an hour. Cooper describes the ark, but pretty obscurely. In the matter of dimensions "it was little more than a modern canal boat." Let us guess, then, that it was about 140 feet long. It was of "greater breadth than common." Let us guess, then, that it was about sixteen feet wide. This leviathan had been prowling down bends which were but a third as long as itself, and scraping between banks where it had only two feet of space to spare on each side. We cannot too much admire this miracle. A low-roofed log dwelling occupies "two-thirds of the ark's length"—a dwelling ninety feet long and sixteen feet wide, let us say—a kind of vestibule train. The dwelling has two rooms—each forty-five feet long and sixteen feet wide, let us guess. One of them is the bed-room of the Hutter girls, Judith and Hetty; the other is the parlor, in the day time, at night it is papa's bed chamber. The ark is arriving at the stream's exit, now, whose width has been reduced to less than twenty feet to accommodate the Indians—say to eighteen. There is a foot to spare on each side of the boat. Did the Indians notice that there was going to be a tight squeeze there? Did they notice that they could make money by climbing down out of that arched sapling and just stepping aboard when the ark scraped by? No; other Indians would have noticed these things, but Cooper's Indians never notice anything. Cooper thinks they are marvellous creatures for noticing, but he was almost always in error about his Indians. There was seldom a sane one among them.

The ark is 140 feet long; the dwelling is 90 feet long. The idea of the Indians is to drop softly and secretly from the arched sapling to the dwelling as the ark creeps along under it at the rate of a mile an hour, and butcher the family. It will take the ark a minute and a half to pass under. It will take the 90-foot dwelling a minute to pass under. Now, then, what did the six Indians do? It would take you thirty years to guess, and even then you would have to give it up, I believe. Therefore, I will tell you what the Indians did. Their chief, a person of quite extraordinary intellect for a Cooper Indian, warily watched the canal boat as it squeezed along under him, and when he had got his calculations fined down to exactly the right shade, as he judged, he let go and dropped. And *missed the house!* That is actually what he did. He missed the house, and landed in the stern of the scow. It was not much of a fall, yet it knocked him silly. He lay there unconscious. If the house had been 97 feet long, he would have made the trip. The fault was Cooper's, not his. The error lay in the construction of the house. Cooper was no architect.

There still remained in the roost five Indians. The boat has passed under and is now out of their reach. Let me explain what the five did—you would not be able to reason it out for yourself. No. 1 jumped for the boat, but fell in the water astern of it. Then No. 2 jumped for the boat, but fell in the water still further astern of it. Then No. 3 jumped for the boat, and fell a good way astern of it. Then No. 4 jumped for the boat, and fell in the water *away* astern. Then even No. 5 made a jump for the boat—for he was a Cooper Indian. In the matter of intellect, the difference between a Cooper Indian and the Indian that stands in front of the cigar shop is not spacious. The scow episode is really a sublime burst of invention; but it does not thrill, because the inaccuracy of the details throws a sort of air of fictitiousness and general improbability over it. This comes of Cooper's inadequacy as an observer.

The reader will find some examples of Cooper's high talent for inaccurate observation in the account of the shooting match in *The Pathfinder*. "A common wrought nail was driven lightly into the target, its head having been first touched with paint." The color of the paint is not stated—an important omission, but Cooper deals freely in important omissions. No, after all, it was not an important omission; for this nail head is *a hundred yards* from the marksman and could not be seen by them at that distance no matter what its color might be. How far can the best eyes see a common house fly? A hundred yards? It is quite impossible. Very well, eyes that cannot see a house fly that is a hundred yards away cannot see an ordinary nail head at that distance, for the size of the two objects is the same. It takes a keen eye to see a fly or a nail head at fifty yards—one hundred and fifty feet. Can the reader do it?

The nail was lightly driven, its head painted, and game called. Then the Cooper miracles began. The bullet of the first marksman chipped an edge of the nail head; the next man's bullet drove the nail a little way into the target—and removed all the paint. Haven't the miracles gone far enough now? Not to suit Cooper; for the purpose of this whole scheme is to show off his prodigy, Deerslayer-Hawkeye-Long-Rifle-Leather-Stocking-Pathfinder-Bumppo before the ladies.

"Be all ready to clench it, boys!" cried out Pathfinder, stepping into his friend's tracks the instant they were vacant. "Never mind a new nail; I can see that, though the paint is gone, and what I can see, I can hit at a hundred yards, though it were only a mosquitoe's eye. Be ready to clench!"

The rifle cracked, the bullet sped its way and the head of the nail was buried in the wood, covered by the piece of flattened lead.

There, you see, is a man who could hunt flies with a rifle, and command a ducal salary in a Wild West show to-day, if we had him back with us.

The recorded feat is certainly surprising, just as it stands; but it is not surprising enough for Cooper. Cooper adds a touch. He has made Pathfinder do this miracle with another man's rifle, and not only that, but

Pathfinder did not have even the advantage of loading it himself. He had everything against him, and yet he made that impossible shot, and not only made it, but did it with absolute confidence, saying, "Be ready to clench." Now a person like that would have undertaken that same feat with a brickbat, and with Cooper to help he would have achieved it, too.

Pathfinder showed off handsomely that day before the ladies. His very first feat was a thing which no Wild West show can touch. He was standing with the group of marksmen, observing—a hundred yards from the target, mind: one Jasper raised his rifle and drove the centre of the bull's-eye. Then the quartermaster fired. The target exhibited no result this time. There was a laugh. "It's a dead miss," said Major Lundie. Pathfinder waited an impressive moment or two, then said in that calm, indifferent, know-it-all way of his, "No, Major—he has covered Jasper's bullet, as will be seen if any one will take the trouble to examine the target."

Wasn't it remarkable! How *could* he see that little pellet fly through the air and enter that distant bullet-hole? Yet that is what he did; for nothing is impossible to a Cooper person. Did any of those people have any deep-seated doubts about this thing? No; for that would imply sanity, and these were all Cooper people.

The respect for Pathfinder's skill and for his *quickness and accuracy of sight* (the italics are mine) was so profound and general, that the instant he made this declaration the spectators began to distrust their own opinions, and a dozen rushed to the target in order to ascertain the fact. There, sure enough, it was found that the quartermaster's bullet had gone through the hole made by Jasper's, and that, too, so accurately as to require a minute examination to be certain of the circumstance, which, however, was soon clearly established by discovering one bullet over the other in the stump against which the target was placed.

They made a "minute" examination; but never mind, how could they know that there were two bullets in that hole without digging the latest one out? for neither probe nor eyesight could prove the presence of any more than one bullet. Did they dig? No; as we shall see. It is the Pathfinder's turn now; he steps out before the ladies, takes aim, and fires.

But alas! here is a disappointment; an incredible, an unimaginable disappointment—for the target's aspect is unchanged; there is nothing there but that same old bullet hole!

"If one dared to hint at such a thing," cried Major Duncan, "I should say that the Pathfinder has also missed the target."

As nobody had missed it yet, the "also" was not necessary; but never mind about that, for the Pathfinder is going to speak.

"No, no, Major," said he, confidently, "that *would* be a risky declaration. I didn't load the piece, and can't say what was in it, but if it was lead, you will find the bullet driving down those of the Quartermaster and Jasper, else is not my name Pathfinder."

A shout from the target announced the truth of this assertion.

Is the miracle sufficient as it stands? Not for Cooper. The Pathfinder speaks again, as he "now slowly advances towards the stage occupied by the females:"

"That's not all, boys, that's not all; if you find the target touched at all, I'll own to a miss. The Quartermaster cut the wood, but you'll find no wood cut by that last messenger."

The miracle is at last complete. He knew—doubtless *saw*—at the distance of a hundred yards—that his bullet had passed into the hole *without fraying the edges*. There were now three bullets in that one hole—three bullets imbedded processionally in the body of the stump back of the target. Everybody knew this—somehow or other—and yet nobody had dug any of them out to make sure. Cooper is not a close observer, but he is interesting. He is certainly always that, no matter what happens. And he is more interesting when he is not noticing what he is about than when he is. This is a considerable merit.

The conversations in the Cooper books have a curious sound in our modern ears. To believe that such talk really ever came out of people's mouths would be to believe that there was a time when time was of no value to a person who thought he had something to say; when it was the custom to spread a two-minute remark out to ten; when a man's mouth was a rolling-mill, and busied itself all day long in turning four-foot pigs of thought into thirty-foot bars of conversational railroad iron by attenuation; when subjects were seldom faithfully stuck to, but the talk wandered all around and arrived nowhere; when conversations consisted mainly of irrelevances, with here and there a relevancy, a relevancy with an embarrassed look, as not being able to explain how it got there.

Cooper was certainly not a master in the construction of dialogue. Inaccurate observation defeated him here as it defeated him in so many other enterprises of his. He even failed to notice that the man who talks corrupt English six days in the week must and will talk it on the seventh, and can't help himself. In the *Deerslayer* story he lets Deerslayer talk the showiest kind of book talk sometimes, and at other times the basest of base dialects. For instance, when some one asks him if he has a sweetheart, and if so, where she abides, this is his majestic answer:

"She's in the forest—hanging from the boughs of the trees, in a soft rain—in the dew on the open grass—the clouds that float about in the blue heavens—the birds that sing in the woods—the sweet springs where I slake my thirst—and in all the other glorious gifts that come from God's Providence!"

And he preceded that, a little before, with this:

"It consarns me as all things that touches a fri'nd consarns a fri'nd."

And this is another of his remarks:

"If I was Injin born, now, I might tell of this, or carry in the scalp and boast of the expl'ite afore the whole tribe; or if my inimy had only been a bear"—and so on.

We cannot imagine such a thing as a veteran Scotch Commander-in-Chief comporting himself in the field like a windy melodramatic actor, but Cooper could. On one occasion Alice and Cora were being chased by the French through a fog in the neighborhood of their father's fort:

"*Point de quartier aux coquins!*" cried an eager pursuer, who seemed to direct the operations of the enemy.

"Stand firm and be ready, my gallant 60ths!" suddenly exclaimed a voice above them; "wait to see the enemy; fire low, and sweep the glacis."

"Father! father!" exclaimed a piercing cry from out the mist; "it is I! Alice! thy own Elsie! spare, O! save your daughters!"

"Hold!" shouted the former speaker, in the awful tones of parental agony, the sound reaching even to the woods, and rolling back in solemn echo. " 'Tis she! God has restored me my children! Throw open the sally-port; to the field, 60ths, to the field; pull not a trigger, lest ye kill my lambs! Drive off these dogs of France with your steel."

Cooper's word-sense was singularly dull. When a person has a poor ear for music he will flat and sharp right along without knowing it. He keeps near the tune, but it is *not* the tune. When a person has a poor ear for words, the result is a literary flatting and sharping; you perceive what he is intending to say, but you also perceive that he doesn't *say* it. This is Cooper. He was not a word-musician. His ear was satisfied with the *approximate* word. I will furnish some circumstantial evidence in support of this charge. My instances are gathered from half a dozen pages of the tale called *Deerslayer*. He uses "verbal," for "oral"; "precision," for "facility"; "phenomena," for "marvels"; "necessary," for "predetermined"; "unsophisticated," for "primitive"; "preparation," for "expectancy"; "rebuked," for "subdued"; "dependent on," for "resulting from"; "fact," for "condition"; "fact," for "conjecture"; "precaution," for "caution"; "explain," for "determine"; "mortified," for "disappointed"; "meretricious," for "factitious"; "materially," for "considerably"; "decreasing," for "deepening"; "increasing," for "disappearing"; "embedded," for "enclosed"; "treacherous," for "hostile"; "stood," for "stooped"; "softened," for "replaced"; "rejoined," for "remarked"; "situation," for "condition"; "different," for "differing"; "insensible," for "unsentient"; "brevity," for "celerity"; "distrusted," for "suspicious"; "mental imbecility," for "imbecility"; "eyes," for "sight"; "counteracting," for "opposing"; "funeral obsequies," for "obsequies."

There have been daring people in the world who claimed that Cooper could write English, but they are all dead now—all dead but Lounsbury. I don't remember that Lounsbury makes the claim in so many words, still he makes it, for he says that *Deerslayer* is a "pure work of art." Pure, in that connection, means faultless—faultless in all details—and language is a detail. If Mr. Lounsbury had only compared Cooper's English with the English which he writes himself—but it is plain that he didn't; and so it is likely that he imagines until this day that Cooper's is as clean and compact as his own. Now I feel sure, deep down in my heart, that Cooper wrote about the poorest English that exists in our language, and that the English of *Deerslayer* is the very worst that even Cooper ever wrote.

I may be mistaken, but it does seem to me that *Deerslayer* is not a work of art in any sense; it does seem to me that it is destitute of every detail that goes to the making of a work of art; in truth, it seems to me that *Deerslayer* is just simply a literary *delirium tremens*.

A work of art? It has no invention; it has no order, system, sequence, or result; it has no lifelikeness, no thrill, no stir, no seeming of reality; its characters are confusedly drawn, and by their acts and words they prove that they are not the sort of people the author claims that they are; its humor is pathetic; its pathos is funny; its conversations are—oh! indescribable; its love-scenes odious; its English a crime against the language.

Counting these out, what is left is Art. I think we must all admit that.

How to Tell a Story

THE HUMOROUS STORY AN AMERICAN DEVELOPMENT. — ITS DIFFERENCE FROM COMIC AND WITTY STORIES.

I DO NOT CLAIM that I can tell a story as it ought to be told. I only claim to know how a story ought to be told, for I have been almost daily in the company of the most expert story-tellers for many years.

There are several kinds of stories, but only one difficult kind—the humorous. I will talk mainly about that one. The humorous story is American, the comic story is English, the witty story is French. The humorous story depends for its effect upon the *manner* of the telling; the comic story and the witty story upon the *matter*.

The humorous story may be spun out to great length, and may wander around as much as it pleases, and arrive nowhere in particular; but the comic and witty stories must be brief and end with a point. The humorous story bubbles gently along, the others burst.

The humorous story is strictly a work of art,—high and delicate art,—and only an artist can tell it; but no art is necessary in telling the comic and the witty story; anybody can do it. The art of telling a humorous story—understand, I mean by word of mouth, not print—was created in America, and has remained at home.

The humorous story is told gravely; the teller does his best to conceal the fact that he even dimly suspects that there is anything funny about it; but the teller of the comic story tells you beforehand that it is one of the funniest things he has ever heard, then tells it with eager delight, and is the first person to laugh when he gets through. And sometimes, if he has had good success, he is so glad and happy that he will repeat the "nub" of it and glance around from face to face, collecting applause, and then repeat it again. It is a pathetic thing to see.

Very often, of course, the rambling and disjointed humorous story finishes with a nub, point, snapper, or whatever you like to call it. Then the listener must be alert, for in many cases the teller will divert attention from that nub by dropping it in a carefully casual and indifferent way, with the pretence that he does not know it is a nub.

Artemus Ward used that trick a good deal; then when the belated audience presently caught the joke he would look up with innocent surprise, as if wondering what they had found to laugh at. Dan Setchell used it before him, Nye and Riley and others use it to-day.

But the teller of the comic story does not slur the nub; he shouts it at you — every time. And when he prints it, in England, France, Germany and Italy, he italicises it, puts some whooping exclamation-points after it, and sometimes explains it in a parenthesis. All of which is very depressing, and makes one want to renounce joking and lead a better life.

Let me set down an instance of the comic method, using an anecdote which has been popular all over the world for twelve or fifteen hundred years. The teller tells it in this way:

The Wounded Soldier.

In the course of a certain battle a soldier whose leg had been shot off appealed to another soldier who was hurrying by to carry him to the rear, informing him at the same time of the loss which he had sustained; whereupon the generous son of Mars, shouldering the unfortunate, proceeded to carry out his desire. The bullets and cannon-balls were flying in all directions, and presently one of the latter took the wounded man's head off — without, however, his deliverer being aware of it. In no long time he was hailed by an officer, who said:

"Where are you going with that carcass?"

"To the rear, sir — he's lost his leg!"

"His leg, forsooth?" responded the astonished officer; "you mean his head, you booby."

Whereupon the soldier dispossessed himself of his burden, and stood looking down upon it in great perplexity. At length he said:

"It is true, sir, just as you have said." Then after a pause he added, *"But he* TOLD *me* IT WAS HIS LEG!!!!!"

Here the narrator bursts into explosion after explosion of thunderous horse-laughter, repeating that nub from time to time through his gaspings and shriekings and suffocatings.

It takes only a minute and a half to tell that in its comic-story form; and isn't worth the telling, after all. Put into the humorous-story form it takes ten minutes, and is about the funniest thing I have ever listened to—as James Whitcomb Riley tells it.

He tells it in the character of a dull-witted old farmer who has just heard it for the first time, thinks it is unspeakably funny, and is trying to repeat it to a neighbor. But he can't remember it; so he gets it all mixed up and wanders helplessly round and round, putting in tedious details that don't belong in the tale and only retard it; taking them out conscientiously and putting in others that are just as useless; making minor mistakes now and then and stopping to correct them and explain how he came to make them; remembering things which he forgot to put in in their proper place and going back to put them in there; stopping his narrative a good while in order to try to recall the name of the soldier that was hurt, and finally remembering that the soldier's name was not mentioned, and remarking placidly that the name is of no real importance, any way,—better, of course, if one knew it, but not essential, after all,—and so on, and so on, and so on.

The teller is innocent and happy and pleased with himself, and has to stop every little while to hold himself in and keep from laughing outright; and does hold in, but his body quakes in a jelly-like way with interior chuckles; and at the end of the ten minutes the audience have laughed until they are exhausted, and the tears are running down their faces.

The simplicity and innocence and sincerity and unconsciousness of the old farmer are perfectly simulated, and the result is a performance which is thoroughly charming and delicious. This is art—and fine and beautiful, and only a master can compass it; but a machine could tell the other story.

To string incongruities and absurdities together in a wandering and sometimes purposeless way, and seem innocently unaware that they are absurdities, is the basis of the American art, if my position is correct.

Another feature is the slurring of the point. A third is the dropping of a studied remark apparently without knowing it, as if one were thinking aloud. The fourth and last is the pause.

Artemus Ward dealt in numbers three and four a good deal. He would begin to tell with great animation something which he seemed to think was wonderful; then lose confidence, and after an apparently absent-minded pause add an incongruous remark in a soliloquizing way; and that was the remark intended to explode the mine—and it did.

For instance, he would say eagerly, excitedly, "I once knew a man in New Zealand who hadn't a tooth in his head"—here his animation would die out; a silent, reflective pause would follow, then he would say dreamily, and as if to himself, "and yet that man could beat a drum better than any man I ever saw."

The pause is an exceedingly important feature in any kind of story, and a frequently recurring feature, too. It is a dainty thing, and delicate, and also uncertain and treacherous; for it must be exactly the right length—no more and no less—or it fails of its purpose and makes trouble. If the pause is too short the impressive point is passed, and the audience have had time to divine that a surprise is intended—and then you can't surprise them, of course.

On the platform I used to tell a negro ghost story that had a pause in front of the snapper on the end, and that pause was the most important thing in the whole story. If I got it the right length precisely, I could spring the finishing ejaculation with effect enough to make some impressible girl deliver a startled little yelp and jump out of her seat—and that was what I was after. This story was called "The Golden Arm," and was told in this fashion. You can practise with it yourself—and mind you look out for the pause and get it right.

The Golden Arm.

Once 'pon a time dey wuz a monsus mean man, en he live 'way out in de prairie all 'lone by hisself, 'cep'n he had a wife. En bimeby she died, en he tuck en toted her way out dah in de prairie en buried her. Well, she had a golden arm—all solid gold, fum de shoulder down. He wuz pow'ful mean—pow'ful; en dat night he couldn't sleep, caze he want dat golden arm so bad.

When it come midnight he couldn't stan' it no mo'; so he git up, he did, en tuck his lantern en shoved out thoo de storm en dug her up en got de golden arm; en he bent his head down 'gin de win', en plowed en plowed en plowed thoo de snow. Den all on a sudden he stop (make a considerable pause here, and look startled, and take a listening attitude) en say: "My *lan'*, what's dat!"

En he listen—en listen—en de win' say (set your teeth together and imitate the wailing and wheezing singsong of the wind), "Bzzz-z-zzz"—en den, way back yonder whah de grave is, he hear a *voice!*—he hear a voice all mix' up in de win'—can't hardly tell 'em 'part—"Bzzz-zzz—W-h-o—g-o-t—m-y—g-o-l-d-e-n *arm?*—zzz—zzz—W-h-o g-o-t m-y g-o-l-d-e-n *arm?*" (You must begin to shiver violently now.)

En he begin to shiver en shake, en say, "Oh, my! *Oh*, my lan'!" en de win' blow de lantern out, en de snow en sleet blow in his face en mos' choke him, en he start a-plowin' knee-deep toward home mos' dead, he so sk'yerd—en pooty soon he hear de voice agin, en (pause) it 'us comin' *after* him! "Bzzz—zzz—zzz—W-h-o—g-o-t—m-y g-o-l-d-e-n—*arm?*"

When he git to de pasture he hear it agin—closter now, en a-*comin'*!—a-comin' back dah in de dark en de storm—(repeat the wind and the voice). When he git to de house he rush up-stairs en jump in de bed en kiver up, head and years, en lay dah shiverin' en shakin'—en den way out dah he hear it *agin!*—en a-*comin'*! En bimeby he hear (pause—awed, listening attitude)—pat—pat—pat—*hit's* a-comin' up-stairs! Den he hear de latch, en he *know* it's in de room!

Den pooty soon he know it's a-*stannin' by de bed!* (Pause.) Den—he know it's a—*bendin' down over him*—en he cain't skasely git his breath! Den—den—he seem to feel someth'n *c-o-l-d*, right down 'most agin his head! (Pause.)

Den de voice say, *right at his year*—"W-h-o—g-o-t—m-y—g-o-l-d-e-n *arm?*" (You must wail it out very plaintively and accusingly; then you stare steadily and impressively into the face of the farthest-gone audi-tor,—a girl, preferably,—and let that awe-inspiring pause begin to build itself in the deep hush. When it has reached exactly the right length, jump suddenly at that girl and yell, "*You've* got it!"

If you've got the *pause* right, she'll fetch a dear little yelp and spring right out of her shoes. But you *must* get the pause right; and you will find it the most troublesome and aggravating and uncertain thing you ever undertook.)